MW00624463

Tł
Broken Absolutes
from the epic fantasy series
The Vault of Heaven

"*The Sound of Broken Absolutes* is one of the most beautiful stories I've ever read . . . stunningly gorgeous, painfully intimate, and magnificently epic. This is a story of war, music, loss, and restoration, and it will touch the hearts of its readers."

~The Ranting Dragon

"*The Sound of Broken Absolutes* offers a theme of rebuilding our broken selves. It resonates perfectly. Orullian pours love and dread into his rich novella about art, loss and reconstruction. His tale disturbs and ultimately uplifts with the authenticity only possible from a writer who looked life's hardship in the eye and shook its bony hand."

~PasteMagazine.com

Praise for
The Unremembered
and
Trial of Intentions
Books One & Two of
The Vault of Heaven

"Engaging characters and powerful storytelling in the tradition of Robert Jordan, Terry Goodkind, and Dennis L. McKiernan make this a top-notch fantasy by a new author to watch."

~ *Library Journal* (Starred review)

"A sprawling, complex tale of magic and destiny that won't disappoint its readers. This auspicious beginning for author Peter Orullian will have you looking forward to more." ∼ Terry Brooks

"The Vault of Heaven is an ambitious story in the mold of Robert Jordan and Terry Goodkind. Peter Orullian is a name to watch in the field of epic fantasy." ∼ Kevin J. Anderson

"This is one huge, powerful, compelling, hard-hitting story . . . The Vault of Heaven is a major fantasy adventure." ∼ Piers Anthony

"A fine debut!" ∼ Brandon Sanderson

"Great fantasy tales plunge us into vivid new worlds, in the company of fascinating characters. The Vault of Heaven is great fantasy. It grips you and shows you true friendship, strange places, and heroes growing to confront world-shaking evil. Magnificent! I want more!" ∼ Ed Greenwood

"The Vault of Heaven by Peter Orullian is a vast canvas filled with thought-provoking ideas on the questions of good and evil that engage us all." ∼ Anne Perry

"Intricately crafted with its own distinct melody, *The Unremembered* is a groundbreaking work of epic fantasy." ∼ Bookwormblues.net

"Sometimes you just need a big, fat fantasy, and Peter Orullian's remastered edition of *The Unremembered* delivers everything you're looking for: a fascinating world, tense action, charismatic characters, and a magic system the like of which you've never imagined." ∼ Aidan Moher
A Dribble of Ink
Hugo Award Winner

"*The Unremembered* captures the unique essence and mystery of music, and weaves it into every line of a compelling and exciting world, while telling a character-driven story that resonates through the ages . . . a work of art on par with the masters of the genre, Jordan, Rothfuss, Tolkien, and more."

∼ Elitistbookreviews.com
2013 & 2014 Hugo-nominated
for best review site

"Engaging characters, complex magic, and expertly written—a whole new kind of epic fantasy!"　　　　　∼ Suvudu.com

"*Trial of Intentions* is a story of music and magic, of daring and sacrifice, in an intricate and believable world, where characters face difficult and heartbreaking choices. Orullian is doing things I haven't seen in other books, including an original system of magic. This tale will resonate with readers long after the cover is closed."　　　　　∼ Robin Hobb

"Peter Orullian's *Trial of Intentions* is a book enormous in scope and in intricacy, with a welter of political, cultural, and magical intrigues, behind which lies the role of song in preserving a myriad of cultures, all of which disagree with each other to some extent, even as it becomes apparent to the reader that, without some degree of cooperation, all will suffer, if not perish. A challenging story about challenged cultures, and one well-told."

∼ L. E. Modesitt, Jr.

"Peter Orullian is a master of dark chocolate fantasy; bitter, harsh and sweet at once. *Trial of Intentions* grabs us firmly by the breastplate and challenges us to face a world of moral contradictions, stunning characters and harsh choices. An unflinching fantasy."

∼ Tracy Hickman

Also by Peter Orullian

The Unremembered
Trial of Intentions
The Vault of Heaven, Story Volume One

All is resonance!

THE SOUND OF BROKEN ABSOLUTES

PETER ORULLIAN

descant publishing

The Sound of Broken Absolutes
Copyright © 2015 by Peter Orullian

Cover Art by Rado Javor
Cover Design by Peter Orullian

The Sound of Broken Absolutes *is a work of fiction. All of the characters, orga-nizations, and events portrayed are either products of the author's imagination or are used fictitiously.*

All rights reserved
ISBN 978-0-9712909-3-8

Publication History
First published in Unfettered 2013

Published by
Descant Publishing

10 9 8 7 6 5 4 3 2 1

For Maestro David Kyle,
who taught me far more than music alone

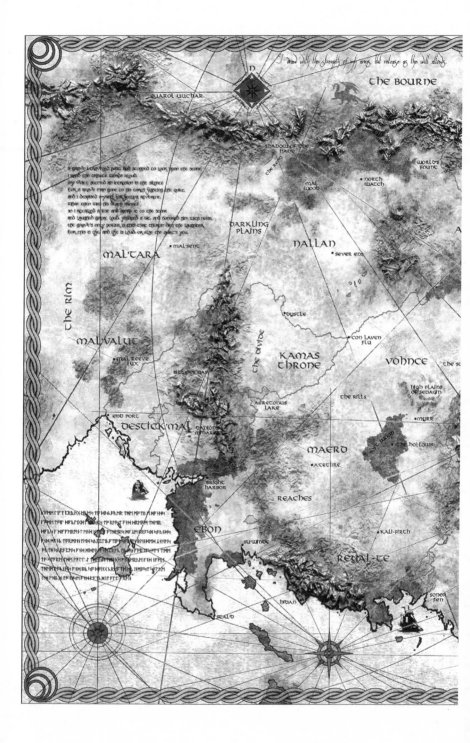

PALL MOUNTAINS

SAECULA FOREST

SO'LIEL STRECKINES

SAECULORUM MOUNTAINS

NALTUS FAR

•NORHAL

SOTOL WASTES

ELYK DIVAD

All the rest we making early harsh fast, employing loudly in journeys

•IR-CAUL

LONITOL

PALECE RANGE

TANGLE WOOD

LUNOL PASS

WYNSTOUT DOMINION

•A'VOTEL

U'TILAT MOR

NALTUS REU

AR

REDTUV

BALENS

KUREN

PATER FUI

For there are two eternal truths that may not be put asunder,
that Force and Forms, or matter, and energy, or body and spirit,
can be neither created nor destroyed only rendered changed, more
than and next that these eternal elements may choose for themselves.

SO'DELL

MAVEN WOOD

DYNLUL MOOR

MASSON DIMN

THE EAST OF
AESHAU VAAL
IN THE AGE OF
RUMOR

•RIVEN PORT

DALLE

SOREN SEAS

INTRODUCTION

MUSIC MATTERS. It matters in real life. And it certainly matters in the world of my fantasy series, The Vault of Heaven.

You may recall the film, Mr. Holland's Opus. I'm cribbing a bit, but during one great scene Richard Dreyfuss says to the principal, who's cutting back the art program: "If you take away music, sooner or later, there'll be nothing to read or write about."

Point and match.

Obviously, I'm biased. Music is a big part of my life. And so it was natural that it made its way into my fiction. Which it does here in *The Sound of Broken Absolutes*. But let me tell you how I came to write this novella.

A friend of mine got cancer. For the second time. On many of his chemotherapy days, I went and sat with him. Just to chat. Keep him company. I know he appreciated it. But at the end of the day, my offering felt small. Because I'd eventually head home after surreal conversations in which we spoke about his chances of beating cancer. Or not.

It reminds me of a dark novel I wrote once (a hard story to write and one I've never tried to publish) that grew out of this idea: The pain and helplessness of watching someone you love die. I wrote a whole concept album around it, too—also unreleased. Maybe that's why I went at this story the way I did. With a kind of reckless abandon. I needed to do something more. Needed to say something this time. (That whole *this time* reference is a long story for another day.)

So I poured myself into it. For weeks. Things that matter to me converged on the page: family, loyalty, friendship, authenticity . . . music. I began telling a story set in the universe of my series. It's the story of two men—one old, one young—each putting his music-craft to use in very different ways.

I imagine you've heard the adage, "Music has charms to sooth a savage breast." Well, the phrase was coined by William Congreve in his play *The Mourning Bride*:

> Musick has Charms to sooth a savage Breast,
> To soften Rocks, or bend a knotted Oak.
> I've read, that things inanimate have mov'd,
> And, as with living Souls, have been inform'd,
> By Magick Numbers and persuasive Sound.
> What then am I? Am I more sensless grown
> Than Trees, of Flint? O force of constant Woe!
> 'Tis not in Harmony to calm my Griefs.
> Anselmo sleeps, and is at Peace; last Night
> The Silent Tomb receiv'd the good old King;
> He and his Sorrows now are safely lodg'd

Within its cold, but hospitable Bosom.

Why am not I at Peace?

I can't even begin to unpack those lines in this short intro. But I'll tell you this: It's no accident that the central song of power in my music magic system is known as The Song of Suffering. And I'll tell you that music in this story sometimes soothes, sometimes moves inanimate things. It has to do with numbers (more on that in book three of The Vault of Heaven). And it has to do with the notion of absolute sound. And harmony. And resonance. To calm grief. One way or another.

This tale was written to stand on its own. Meaning, if you haven't read my novels, you'll be okay digging into *Broken Absolutes*. But if you're reading my series, this is the first really in-depth discussion and use of my music magic system. And it ties really well to book two, *Trial of Intentions*, which—for the uninitiated—was written as an entry point to my series. So, if you like *Broken Absolutes*, it's possible for you to come along on the journey starting with *Trial of Intentions*, where music has a power of its own.

Music matters. It matters in real life. And it certainly matters in the world of my fantasy series.

And as for Richard Dreyfuss' character, Mr. Holland, I think he'd applaud the fact that I'm not done writing about music.

February 2015

Peter Orullian

THE SOUND OF
BROKEN
ABSOLUTES

ONE

MAESTERI DIVAD JONASON gently removed the viola d'amore from its weathered sheepskin case. In the silence, he smiled wanly over the old instrument, considering. *Sometimes the most important music lessons feature no music at all.* Such was the case with this viola, an old friend to be sure. It served a different kind of instruction. One that came late in the training of a Lieholan, whose song had the power of *intention*. This instrument could only be understood when the act of making notes work together had long since been any kind of challenge. This viola made fine music, too, of course—a soft, retiring sound most pleasant in the shades of evening. But this heirloom of the Maesteri, generations old now, taught the kind of resonance often only heard inwardly while standing over a freshly dug barrow.

Behind him, the door opened, and he turned to greet his finest Lieholan student, Belamae Sento. The young man stepped into the room, his face pale, an open letter in his hand. Divad didn't need to ask the contents of the note. In

1

fact, it was the letter's arrival that had hastened his invitation to have Belamae join him in this music chamber.

"Close the door, please." Softly spoken, his words took on a hum-like quality, resounding in the near-perfect acoustics of the room.

Belamae absently did as he was asked. The wide-eyed look on his face was not, Divad knew, amazement at finally coming to the Chamber of Absolutes. Although such would have been normal enough for one of the Lyren—a student of the Descant—it wasn't so for Belamae. Not today. Worry and conflict had taken the young man's thoughts far from Descant Cathedral, far from his focus on learning the Song of Suffering.

"You seem distracted. Does finally coming here leave you at a loss for words?" He raised an open palm to indicate the room, but was really just easing them into conversation.

Belamae looked around and shook his head. "It's less . . . impressive than I'd imagined."

Divad chuckled low in his throat, the sound musical in the resonant chamber. "Quite so. I tend not to correct assumptions about this place. Could be that I like the surprise of it when Lieholan see it with their own eyes. But the last lessons in Suffering are plain ones. The room is rightly spare."

The walls and floor and vaulted ceiling were bare granite. In fact, the only objects in the room were four instruments: a boxharp, a dual-tubed horn, a mandola, and the viola Divad held in his hands. Each had a place in an arched cutaway at equal distances around the circular chamber.

He held up the viola. "What about the instruments? What do they suggest you might learn here?"

Belamae looked around again, more slowly this time, coming last to the viola. He concluded with a shrug.

"Aliquot stringing," Divad said, supplying the answer. "It's resonance, my boy. And leads us to *absolute sound.*"

Belamae nodded, seeming unimpressed or maybe just overly distracted. "Do we have to do this today?"

"Because of the letter you've received," he replied, knowing it was precisely so.

The young Lieholan stared down at the missive in his hands, and spoke without raising his eyes. "I've looked forward to the things you'd teach me here. We all do." He paused, heaving a deep sigh. "But war has come to my people. We're losing the fight. And my da . . . I have to go."

"Aliquots are intentionally unplayed strings that resonate harmonically when you strike the others." He held up the viola and pointed to a second set of seven gut strings strung below those the bow would caress.

Belamae looked up, an incredulous expression on his face.

Divad paid the look no mind. "A string vibrates when struck. There's a mathematical relationship between a vibrating string and an aliquot that resonates with it. This is usually in unison or octaves, but can also come in fifths. We've spoken of resonance before, but always as a way of understanding music that must be *heard* to have a resonant effect."

"Did you hear me?" Belamae asked, irritation edging his voice. "I'm leaving."

"Absolute sound," Divad went on, "is resonance you feel even when it's *not* heard."

"My da—"

"Which is what makes this instrument doubly instructive. You see, we play it in requiem." He caressed the neck of the viola, oiled smooth for easy finger positioning. "Voices sometimes falter, tremulous with emotion. That's understandable. So just as often, we play the dirge with this. And the melody helps to bring the life of a departed loved one into resonance with those they've left behind. Like the sweet grief of memory."

Belamae's anger sharpened. "In requiem . . . You knew my da was dead? And you didn't tell me?"

Divad shook his head. "You're missing the point. There is a music that can connect you with others in a . . . fundamental way. As fundamental as the sound their life makes. And once you find that resonant sound, it surpasses distance. It no longer needs to be heard to have effect."

The young Lieholan glared back at the older man. Then his brow relaxed, disappointment replacing everything else. "You're telling me not to go."

"I'm telling you you're more important to them here, learning to sing Suffering, than you would be in the field as one more man with a sword." He offered a conciliatory smile. "And you're close, my boy. Ready to understand absolute sound. Nearly ready to sing Suffering on your own."

Belamae shook his head. "I won't ignore their call for help. People are dying." He glanced at the viola in Divad's hands. "They wouldn't have sent for me if it was my sword they wanted. But you don't have to worry; I know how to use my song."

"And what song do you think you have, Belamae? The song you came here with?" His tone became suddenly cross. "Or do you pretend you can make Suffering a weapon? That is not its intention. You would bring greater harm to your own people if that's why you go. I won't allow it."

"You're a coward," Belamae replied with the indignation only the young seem capable of. "I will go and do what I—"

"You should let your loss teach you *more* about Suffering, not take you away from it." Divad strummed the viola's strings, then immediately silenced them. The aliquots hummed in the stillness, resonating from the initial vibration of the viola's top seven strings.

The two men stood staring at one another as the aliquots rang on, which was no brief time. Divad knew trying to force Belamae to stay would prove pointless. Crucial to a Descant education was a Lieholan's willingness. Especially with regard to absolute sound. But if he could get Belamae to grasp the concept, then perhaps the boy would be convinced to remain.

Divad reached into his robe and removed a funeral score penned specifically for this viola. It was a challenging, complex piece of music, made more difficult by the seven strings and their aliquot pairs. Even reading it would stretch his young protégé's skill. Divad had written it himself in anticipation of this very meeting, knowing sooner or later Belamae would learn of the trouble back home. Its theme was separation, constructed in a Maerdian mode that hadn't been used for centuries. It made use of minor seconds and grace notes as central parts of the melody. A listener had to wait patiently for a passage or phrase to resolve, otherwise the note selection might be interpreted as the performer misplaying the piece.

Learning to play it would be its own kind of instruction for the musician, precisely because of the instrument's aliquots.

Divad handed the piece of music to Belamae. "Read this when you think you're ready to hear it." He gently tapped his young friend at the temple, suggesting he be in the right frame of mind when he did so.

Then, more gently still, he handed Belamae the viola d'amore. He wanted this Lieholan to know the heft of it, to run his hands over the flaws in the soundboard, to ask about the intricately carved earless head above the pegbox, to pluck the top-strung gut and listen for the resonating strings beneath . . .

Belamae received the instrument as he had the sheet music, giving it a moment of thoughtful regard. But almost immediately a sneer filled his face, and he slammed the viola down hard on the stone floor, shattering it into pieces.

The crush and clatter of old wood and the twang of snapped strings rose around them in a cacophonous din, echoing in the Chamber of Absolutes. Divad's stomach twisted into knots at the sudden loss of the fine old instrument. The d'amore wasn't crafted anymore. It was as much a historical artifact as it was a unique and beautiful instrument for producing music. And of all the aliquot instruments, it had been his favorite. At Divad's mother's wake, his own former Maesteri had played accompaniment on this viola while Divad sang Johen's "Funerary Triad."

He sank to his knees, instinctively gathering the pieces. Above him he heard the viola bow being snapped in half. The instrument's destruction was complete. Divad's ire flashed bright and hot, and escalated fast. His hands, filled with bits of spruce and bone points still tied with gut, began to tremble with an urge he hadn't felt in a very long time.

With what composure and dignity he could maintain, he gently laid the splintered viola back down and stood. "You ungrateful whoreson. Get out of my sight. And by every absent god, pray I don't forget myself and strike the note of your life. Mundane as I might now find it."

He then watched as Belamae left the room, his student having failed to even try and understand absolute sound. Or perhaps the failure had been Divad's. Belamae hadn't been ready, he told himself. That much was true. But Divad hadn't had a choice. He'd known the lad would feel duty-bound to return home. Still, he never imagined it would go this way. Looking down again, he grieved at the ruin of a beautiful voice—the viola—broken, and appearing impossible to mend.

Two

MORNING FROST CRUNCHED under my boots as I crossed the frozen field. Several weeks of barge, schooner, overland carriage, and bay-mount had brought me from Recityv to within walking distance of the battle staging area. And more importantly, the captain's tent. I'd left within the hour of my last meeting with Maesteri Divad, which still played in my mind like a vesper's strain sung by an unpracticed voice. All sour notes misplaced by bad intonation.

I was able now, finally, to leave the memory of it alone, though. Mostly because of the dread that began to fill my gut. I didn't know what to expect. I'd hoped to see my ma first, and my sister, Semera. To have some news. To offer some comfort. Probably to receive some of the same. But long before reaching Jenipol, I'd been intercepted by two tight-lipped drummel-men. It's easy to spot men who make percussion a trade—their arms show every sinew. They escorted me here. That had been an alarmingly short ride. Our enemies had pushed deep into the Mor Nations.

9

The last twenty paces to the tent, my escorts fell back. That didn't do much for my state of mind. I paused a moment at the tent flap, noting where the frost had condensed into droplets from the heat inside the tent. Then I took a long breath and went in.

The air carried the musky smell of warm bodies after a fitful night beneath thick, rough wool. That, and the odor of spent tallow. Four men sat staring down at a low table in the light of two lamps burning a generous amount of wick. They all looked up at me as though I'd interrupted a prayer.

As I started to introduce myself, the man farthest back nodded grimly and said, "Belamae. I didn't think you'd come. Or I should say, I didn't think the Maesteri would permit it."

His name escaped me, but not his rank—this man held field command. I could tell by the deliberate and careful scarification on the left side of his neck in the form of an inverted T. Four horizontal hash marks crossed the vertical line. They weren't formal signifiers of rank. The Inverted T was a kind of music staff—an old one, a Kylian notation. The number of lines across it indicated the number of octaves the man had mastered. Which would include complete facility in all scales *and* modes across each. It was breadth as well as depth. More than simply impressive. A second scar-line beneath the bottom one meant he could make good use of steel, too.

The men at his table had similar neck scars, but all with one fewer hash. One of these craned his head around, the act seeming to cause him considerable pain. I could see that he'd lost the service of one eye but took no care to cover the wound. A flap of lid hung like a creased drape over the hole.

The one-eyed man looked me up and down the way a tiller does a draft horse just before plow season. "Doesn't look like much. Neck is thin. Skin's soft. He's not used to making sound on open air. He'll quit in three days. Doesn't matter if he's Karll's boy. I don't believe none in loinfruits."

A third man looked on, carefully appraising, but in a different way. The fellow looked up for a moment, as though framing a question. When he stared at me, his gaze was focused, the way Maesteri Divad's became when he watched for truthful answers and understanding. "Do you want a sword?"

I stared back, somewhat puzzled. "That's not why you sent for me."

The last man at the table did not speak, but instead invited me forward with a nod. As I drew close, I saw what the four had been studying. Not terrain or position maps. Not inventory manifests. Not even letters of command and inquiry sent from the seat of the Tilatian king.

Across the table were spread innumerable scores. These leaders of war were sifting sheet music to prepare for the day's battle. In my few years away from home, I'd learned this was uncommon. The Tilatians might be the only people to do it, in fact. And even among my own kind, it hadn't been done in more than three generations.

Coming a step closer, and as I looked into the faces of the men around the table, it wasn't the carefree good humor of conservatory instructors that I saw. Lord knows I'd come across a cartload of those in my travels as a student from Descant Cathedral. No, these were sober-minded men, reviewing the language of song written for an unfortunate purpose. The tent held the cheerless feel of an overcast winter sky.

Sullen, I thought. *Bitter maybe. But sullen for sure.*

"Nine of ten bear steel into battle. There's no shame in that." The field leader sniffed, refocusing on a score laid out in front of him. "But you're right. That's not why we ask you here. Sit down."

I pulled forward a thin barrel and sat next to the captain, as he set before me a stack of music. "What?"

"I'm Baylet. This is Holis, Shem, and Palandas. These," he gently tapped the scores piled loosely before me, "are airs we send to the line. Tell us which one you'll use."

A chair creaked as Holis, the man with one eye, leaned forward, turning a bit sideways to have a good view of the stack.

"We've already selected morale songs to encourage those who carry steel," Baylet added. "Holis has a good eye for that."

The men exchanged scant looks of mirth, as if the joke were as tired as the men themselves.

"Shem's put aside for later a song of comfort and well-being. Something he wrote himself."

"Calimbaer," I muttered, recalling the class of Mor song that accompanied medical treatment.

Baylet looked across at Shem. "He's also found a good sotto voce for Contentment."

I knew that class of song, too. Two classes really. Sotto voce, an incredibly difficult technique to master, in which singing happened almost under the breath. But *Contentment* . . . it was a type of song sung to one who is beyond help, one who can only be given a spot of peace before going to his final earth.

Holis and Shem produced the music Baylet had spoken of, and dropped it on top of the pile before me. I fanned them out and began to scan. The morale song read like a blaze of horns—written for four voices with two soaring lines above a strong set of rhythmic chants beneath. I could hear the mettle and resolve in my mind as I tracked the chord progressions.

Shem's Calimbaer was an elegant piece composed of few notes, each with long sustain. The movement was languid and would be rendered in a thick legato.

But it was the sotto voce piece that really got to me. I sat poring over the note selection, which made brilliant use of the Lydian and Lochrian modes, the composition effortlessly transitioning between the two. It had me taking deep relaxing breaths. Parts of the melody, even just scanning them, instantly evoked simple, forgotten memories. In those moments, I recalled the marble bench on which I sat the first time I kissed a woman. How cool it had been to the touch, contrasted with the heat in my mouth. I then remembered kneeling in my mother's garden, dutifully clearing the weeds, when

I spontaneously created my first real song, or at least the first one I could still recall. And last to my mind came the memory of lying awake, scared, in my first alone-bed, until I heard the comforting, safe sounds of adult voices talking in the outer room.

Baylet swept those selections aside and tapped the original stack again. "Mors who have *influence* in their voice." He gave me a pointed look. "Mors like you. Have each been sent to different lines so that only the Sellari will hear their song. And suffer by it."

The field leader then began to hum a deep pitch, a full octave lower than any note I could reach. The sound of it filled the tent. He gently lifted the topmost score, written on a pressed parchment, and placed it in my hand. When he stopped singing the single note, the silence that followed felt wide and empty, like the bare-limb stretches of late autumn.

He let that silence hang for a long moment before saying, "This is what they will sing today. They have already set out. You should choose quickly."

It wasn't the urgent request or the song he'd sung or the lingering sotto voce that left me in a panic. I put the score aside and began to leaf through the rest of the stack. While I got the impression that the chests I saw in the shadowed corners of the tent carried more music, the fifty or so here would prove to be enough.

Some were reproductions on newer, cleaner paper that still smelled of ink. Most of these were Jollen Caero songs, very old. Jollen was a composer thought to have come down out of the Pall when my Inveterae ancestors had escaped the Bourne. Any other time, I would have liked to study these longer; the melodic choices were as unpredictable as the vocal rhythms. Other selections had been transcribed on parchment that looked like it had seen the field before—ratted edges and smudges where dirty thumbs had held them. Many of these were as interesting as the Jollen songs but for an entirely different reason: their composers were not generally known. And until now, I'd never seen the full scores—only snippets had survived in the forms of childhood rhymes and song-taunts. Seeing the full context for phrases I'd sung here and there all my life left me feeling a bit ashamed and naive.

Before I'd left to study with the Maesteri at Descant, I could have read maybe half of these scores. Back then, I was fluent in six different types of music notation. Now I could read more than thirty. Some of the music here was just that, music only. No lyrics. The Lieholan singing these scores was free to sing them using vowels of his choosing, so long as he didn't attempt to sing actual words.

Other songs in the stack were nothing more than lyrics, but so familiar that any Lieholan worth his brack would know them. The harder part with these came in the language. They hadn't been translated. I counted at least four different languages: early Morian, a difficult Pall tongue, lower Masi, and a root language we knew as Borren. Most

Lieholan would perform these phonetically, singing words they didn't understand. For my part, having spent four years at Descant, where language study went along with music training, I could make out the meaning in the lyrics. These were terrifying words. There'd been little effort at rhyme in them. The worst was a litany of tragic images with no narrative or resolution. It might have been the darkest thing I'd ever read. Something I couldn't *unread*.

I scanned from one sheet to the next, moving from standard Mor notation, to the subdominant axis approach typified on the necks of the men around me, to a symbol-centered system that referred to a mandola neck, to the more elegant Petruc signifier, where slight serifs and swoops on a handful of characters gave the singer all the information he needed to render the pitch. I liked the Petruc system best. Those delicate strokes could be added to written language, allowing the lyrics to become the central part of the piece, while subtle Petruc ornamentation on its letters carried the melodic direction. Originally, it had been created as a code, back during the War of the First Promise.

Probably the most interesting music, though, was a pair of songs written in an augmented Phrygian mode. They were unattributed, but the parchment was old and the Sotol music notation fading some. This music would require vocal gymnastics to carry off, and two voices besides. Though separately composed, they were clearly a call-and-response orchestration. In my mind I could hear where notes sounded together and where vocal runs built tension on top of beautifully dark counterpoint. I wanted to sing this song, whose first bridge was the only portion I had ever heard, and then only the caller side of the arrangement.

All of them I'd heard or sung, if only in part. But the familiarity was precisely the problem and the thing that alarmed me.

When I'd made sure there was nothing *un*familiar, I looked up and locked eyes with Baylet. "You haven't brought the Mor Refrains with you?"

Holis laughed, the squint of his eyes as he did so pinching the lid of his eyeless socket into a pouch of skin. "I see now. You think that's why we called you back. To sing the Refrains. Ah, sapling, we've had it more bitter than this, and not fallen to such foolish desperation." His one remaining eye widened, the way it might if he'd happened on some realization. "But your asking tells us something about you, I think."

The captain knocked on the tabletop once to silence them. "The field men have already marched. Are you rested enough? And is there one of these you know by rote?"

My heart ran cold. They meant to send me to the field ... today. I stood there, struck dumb for a long moment before nodding.

Baylet seemed satisfied and stood. He motioned for me to follow, and I'd just started after him when a hand caught me tightly by the wrist. I looked down to find Palandas holding me. His grip seemed unusually strong for a man his age.

"The best song, when singing the end of someone, is the one you can make while watching him die." He moistened his lips with his tongue. "That'll be one you must know awfully well, my young friend. Since your voice will have to carry on when the rest of you would rather not."

Palandas held me until I nodded my understanding, which I did without any idea what he really meant. He let me go, and I followed Baylet through the tent flap and south across the frozen field. The promise of sun had grown in the east as a faint line of light blue.

We gathered our mounts at the tree line, and the field leader led me south and east through an elm and broad-pine wood. For the better part of a league we rode. As the trees began to thin, he pulled up and dismounted. I slid from the saddle and stood beside him. The shanks of our mounts steamed in the morning chill.

Finally, I couldn't hold it back any longer. "Why haven't you brought the Mor Refrains? The letter I received made it sound dire."

"War is always dire," he said flatly.

"I came through Talonas, Cyr, and Weilend. All burned. All empty. My history isn't strong, but I don't remember us ever losing three cities to those from across the Soren." My breath plumed before my face as I spoke. "Asking me to leave Descant. I assumed you needed someone—"

"Your training is complete then?" Baylet asked, one eyebrow arching.

"No," I admitted. "But the Refrains haven't been sung in so long. I assumed you'd want someone—"

"The Refrains have *never* been sung." His voice held a pinch of reproach. "The first Mors brought them out of the Bourne to *keep* them from being sung. Which the Quiet would surely have done, if they'd ever gotten their hands on them."

"It's why the Sellari come," I said, stating the obvious. "It's why they've always come. If we fail, they won't hesitate to sing them."

Baylet turned to face me. His stare chilled me deeper than the frigid air. "Then don't fail." He pointed ahead. "Twenty Shoarden men wait for you at the tree line."

Shoarden men. As a child, I'd thought Shoarden simply meant "deaf." Later, when I began to study the Borren root tongues, I learned that it meant "to sacrifice sound."

"Shoarden," I muttered to myself.

"Most Lieholan aren't skilled enough to have their song resonate with a specific individual or . . ." he looked away to the south, where the Sellari camped, "group or army or . . . race." He looked back at me. "It's a technique of absolute sound. A technique you'll possess once your training at Descant is complete. Until then, your song affects any who hear it. So, some of the men sacrifice their hearing in order to guard Lieholan in the field. They take the name Shoarden. Today, I've assigned twenty such men to you. Beyond the tree line, a thousand strides or so, the Sellari eastern flank is camped. They'll come hard. Don't let them through."

He'd apparently said all he meant to say, and quickly mounted.

I struggled to remember the thing I'd wanted to ask him. A hundred questions about the Refrains clouded my mind, but I mentally grasped it before he rode away. "My da."

Baylet held his reins steady, staring ahead. "His sword sang, Belamae. Any man who stood beside him in battle would say the same." He then turned to look at me. "Karll was a friend. Proud as hell of you. He'd be angry with me for sending for you. But a son has to . . . Quiet and Chorus, son, if I'd lost my da I'd want to return murder on the bastards. Thought you'd want the same opportunity. Besides that, we need you. We're outnumbered . . ." His eyes, if it was possible, looked suddenly stonier. "Don't fail."

It was a command. But it was also a plea. The desire to step into the breach for my people filled me like a rush of warm wind. It's hard to explain that feeling. The other thing that was true was that Baylet had put the perfect words on the quiet reason inside me that had brought me here: *return murder on the bastards.* I wasn't proud of that feeling, but I couldn't deny it either. And in the end, I didn't find a thing wrong with it.

I started for the tree line before Baylet kicked his mount into a canter. I did not pause when the twenty Shoarden men fell in around me. I did not pause when I came in sight of the first Sellari scout. I did not pause.

And when a hundred, two hundred of the invaders lined the far meadow, coming on with a steady stride, I recalled the music I'd reviewed that morning in the company of four grim men. A dozen of those songs I knew backward and forward. Three times as many other songs I had full command over: lyric, phrasing, rhythm, and melody. Songs that might suit the kind of destructive influence that filled my heart at that moment.

But as the enemy came within earshot, none of these would do. And when I filled my lungs and opened my mouth, only one song came to me. The fifth movement of Suffering: War.

It was a rough-throat song. As all the line-songs shown to me that morning had been. Maesteri Divad liked to smile and say it was "controlled screaming, cultured hollering." That made as much sense as anything else. The intent of these songs was destruction, aggression. Rasping the voice gave it a scouring, abrasive sound. It conveyed violent intent.

I filled my mind with anguish for my da. I recalled the words of the Song of Suffering's War passage. And I let it all burn inside me. Suffering wasn't meant for this purpose, but I was way past caring about that. I let myself feel indignation and hatred against those who had burned my countrymen.

And then I let it all pour from me in a stream of pounding vocal rhythms that shot out like a succession of iron-gloved punches. I didn't know what would happen, but I'd studied *intention* in my Lieholan training. That's a far cry from saying I'd mastered it. But on this chill morning, mine was clear.

The first few Sellari were ripped off their feet and sent crashing hard upon the frozen earth. I'd later remember the puffs of my own hot breath on the cold air as I shouted out Suffering's War music, which had been meant for protection. I'd instinctively found the way to make that music a weapon. It was the difference between winning and not losing; between merely drawing breath and gasping it in after a mad dash. It actually taught me a practical lesson on *intention* in a way my Descant study of the principle never had.

At the far end of the great field, hundreds more Sellari appeared in full dress, rushing forward. The Shoarden tightened their circle around me, taking out runners my song didn't seem to affect. When I saw that these runners' ears had been cut off, I realized the Sellari had Shoarden of their own.

The sight of them only deepened my anger. The song itself began to live inside me in a way it never had at Recityv. The feeling was strange. It buoyed me up. But I was simultaneously aware that it was being fueled by some part of me that I wouldn't get back.

I didn't care.

I lengthened my stride. The next notes rushed up past my throat into the natural cavities behind my nose and cheeks, becoming a bright, powerful scream that I shrieked into the morning light. Thirty more had flesh ripped from their face and hands. I heard necks pop, and saw heads cock at unnatural angles, and then bodies falling to the hard earth.

Every attack made me stronger. And sicker it seemed. Though strangely, the burn of aggression kept me moving forward, each screamed musical line felling more of the others. I was soon walking over the bodies of Sellari, eager to take them all down.

I never got that far. The ill feeling soon outbalanced the vengeance, and I struggled to even take a breath. Before I knew it, the Shoarden had picked me up and were rushing me back across the great field ahead of the chasing Sellari. I blacked out to the sound of rushing feet pounding over brittle ground.

THREE

H E'D LAID THE BROKEN pieces of the viola out across his worktable like pieces of a puzzle. The sun bathed Descant's lutherie, a haven where Maesteri Divad spent as much time as he could afford. Putting his hands to use in repairing broken instruments helped him think. Occasionally he crafted something new. But he much preferred mending what was broken. It allowed him to maintain his sense of an object's intrinsic worth.

As he sat surveying the wreckage, he breathed deeply the scents of birch woodshavings, willow blocks aging nicely against the outer wall, and the Tamber steel of chisels and planes and fine-tipped paring knives. In the sunlight, motes lazed through the stillness, moving ever so slowly.

The viola's single-piece flat-back had taken too much damage from Belamae's smashing of the instrument. It would have to be replaced. The same was true of the side pieces. Divad picked up the inside blocks and soundpost, which appeared intact. He stress-tested them, gently trying to snap them with his fingers. They seemed fine, until two of the blocks broke where hairline cracks gave way. Those might have been there before Belamae's outburst. Regardless, he resolved to replace all these, too. The gut strings, of course, had all snapped. Those would be easily replaced; Divad knew a good abattoir that specialized in gut drawn from young prairie sheep. That would be one element of repairing the viola where he'd use new material.

The tail, bridge, and neck had all cracked visibly. The bone points, pegbox, pegs, and scrollhead were all salvageable. And the fingerboard—a beautiful length of ebony—remained in perfect condition. That didn't surprise him; ebony was strong.

It was the soundboard that worried him most. Besides being the face of the instrument, it was the piece most crucial to producing the sound of the instrument itself. Wood selection would be everything in its repair. But he loved the challenge of it. The work of carefully piecing this fine old viola back together would be a welcome distraction from the predicament of there being too few Lieholan to sing Suffering. It might also take his mind off the investigation the League of Civility had begun to make of Descant and its Maesteri.

Divad sighed heavily in the quiet of the luthier shop, then smiled to himself. *Living would mean nothing without burden.*

With that thought, he got up and crossed to the racks of wood used for building and repairing woodwinds and stringed instruments. An entire shelf of bird's-eye maple sat in the cool shade on that side of the room. The shelf tag indicated that it had been cut in the forest of Pater Fol one hundred fifty-eight years ago. That'd do nicely for the back. He also found a shelf of willow taken from the Cantle Wood in Alon I'tol. This wood was fresher, a few years old, but would do just fine. It was lightweight, strong, and difficult to split—perfect for the blocks, which took a lot of stress.

As for the soundboard, Descant kept two shelves of old-cut red spruce. They had several different harvest years of the wood, all from the Mor coastal alps: sixty-one years old, one hundred twelve years old, and a short shelf with a tag reading H.G. 481. H.G., Hargrove, was the current age, so named for the poet. This spruce harvest was almost two hundred ninety years old. More than good.

But when it came to repair, Divad went on instinct as much as anything else. Every other component *felt* right: the bird's-eye maple, the willow, the remaining bits that hadn't taken any damage. But for the soundboard . . . he'd have to keep looking. This was no ordinary instrument. He knew of no replica. It accompanied the Johen triad. It was his best tool for teaching the resonance of absolute sound. The soundboard wood needed to be tried and tested. Regardless its age, any wood he had here in his shop would be like a sapling that bends and pulls free in a rough wind.

But Divad had no ready answer for where next to look. He had savvy contacts in the timber trade, of course. They might have suggestions for him. And he knew other luthiers in the city, as well as several more in the eastlands. But he tired at the thought of having to journey to call on them. And he couldn't afford to be away from Descant anyway. So, he went where he always did when he needed to think.

He shrugged into his cloak and slipped through the streets of the Cathedral quarter and into a lesser-known performance tavern called Rafters. Coming here was a holdover from the time before he, himself, had entered Descant to train. Lulling conversation over a mild glass of wheat bitter always mellowed him to the point of inspiration.

Rafters was on a small lane far from the nearest major thoroughfare. Committed drinkers rarely found their way here, since there were closer places to start their binge. And they wouldn't have come for the music, since music didn't factor much in a drinker's decision on where to begin. But musicians were a different tribe.

There were numerous performance taverns in Recityv. And truth be told, for the most part anyway, they were all unofficial audition halls for Descant. While Suffering lay at the heart of the cathedral's purpose, there were hundreds of music students there who would never lay eyes on its music. Some harbored dreams of one day singing Suffering or maybe becoming Maesteri themselves. But most of them understood the reality of those aspirations, and had come to the Cathedral for its unequaled music training. Musicians who cared about the craft all wanted admission. However, there was no formal process for that. Divad could accept a petition to become Lyren from anyone for any reason. Belamae had shown up from Y'Tilat Mor four years ago and done nothing more than hand him a self-drawn diagram of the circle of fifths and shared with him a model for altering it to produce a lovely dissonance. It had also been nice to learn he could "sing from his ass," as the saying went. The kid had one hell of a voice.

Over time, and in the absence of a defined path, Recityv performance taverns had become the best way to build recognition for musical prowess. On any given night, Divad might hear a lap or floor harp, kanteles, psalteries, lutes, flutes, zithers, horns, cellos, violins, hand drums, chimes. And those who sang: soloists, ensembles, choirs, duets, tenors, altos, contraltos, sopranos, and so on.

The taverns on the main roads were pay-to-play. Musicians actually handed over a fee to the proprietor for fifteen minutes of stage time. The going rate stood at three plugs. The larger houses got four.

Rafters didn't take money for stage time. But you didn't just show up and have your name added to the stage-side slate, either. In rare instances, you could play something for Ollie, the proprietor-bouncer-barkeep-and-gossip-curator, in private impromptu auditions. He'd been known to let an act or two play on raw talent alone. But most of those who took the stage had earned the respect of other established musicians. And they had followings of their own that came specifically to hear them play. Such clientele were less likely to wind up in a brawl or putting illicit hands on barmaids. Ollie curated his crowds as much as he did good rumors.

Which wasn't to say it didn't get lively at Rafters. Divad took great pleasure in watching the musicians' skill whip the crowds here into a frenzy. It reminded him that music had a power all its own, well before the gifts of a Lieholan's intention gave it influence.

He arrived ahead of the evening crowd. Regulars had already staked out their places—Chom, who'd been a promising violinist before a mill accident took his hand; Jaela, who cared mostly for the vocalists, having abandoned her own musical ambitions years ago when Divad let her know she was tone-deaf; Riddol and Mack, a pair of genial-enough fellows, as long as the music proved truly satisfying—they were fair but harsh critics. Divad nodded to them all, receiving enthusiastic acknowledgments—Maesteri in the house meant players would push themselves tonight.

He climbed onto his stool at the far end of the bar near the stage, and rubbed a bit of weariness from his face. Much as the prospect of rebuilding the viola excited him, another part of him felt the constant pull of worry and regret over Belamae's departure. Odds were the lad would not survive his country's war. A damn shame, that.

Before he could spend too much energy on the dismal thought, Ollie stood before him, a damp towel slung over his shoulder, ready to mop up a spill.

"Wheat bitter tonight?" Ollie gave him a close look. "Or are you here to drink heavy. Push out some of what's botherin' ya?"

"What makes you think something's bothering me?" Divad replied.

Ollie just gave him an are-you-serious look.

"Wheat bitter'll do." Divad glanced up at the stage-side slate. "Who you got tonight?"

"Madalin is back in the city. She wants to sing something she wrote herself while down in Dimn. She won't preview it for me. Told her she can live or die by it then. She'll probably bring the house down. Woman's got lungs."

Divad nodded. "That she does. I see Colas. Is he playing alone?"

Ollie gave a wry smile. "Oh that. Yeah, Senchia took a lover. Her lines have gravitated to droning chordal roots. Colas is better off without her. He's striking too hard though. I think he's trying to fill up the same amount of sound without her. He'll figure it out. He's slinging new wood, too."

The reference reminded Divad of his reason for coming to Rafters: to think, ponder how to tackle the viola sound-board. While he got himself refocused, Ollie slid a glass of So-Dell light grain in front of him.

"Tell me how that does ya." Ollie smiled with bartender satisfaction. "Came in about a cycle back, but it's a full nine years aged. Wheat was threshed late that season, full ripe kind of taste, if you follow."

Divad took a sip, and his brows rose in pleasant surprise. "Enough of those and *I* might sing tonight."

"You're not on the slate," Ollie said, half kidding. The man liked things planned and proper, but he'd put his towel to a name and write Divad in if he got serious about it.

"I see Alosol is singing last," Divad said, taking a healthier draught off his glass.

"Still the best voice not to be taken into Descant," Ollie observed, giving him a mock judgmental glare.

Alosol had an immense following, and for good reason. He had more control and range in his tenor voice than almost any vocalist in Recityv. Problem was, he knew it. There was a smidge too much conceit in the man. Maybe more than a smidge. But that took nothing from his sheer ability. He could sustain a note three octaves above speech-tone, and do it as softly or with as much volume as another singer would his first octave. Divad didn't have a student that wasn't envious of Alosol's gift, save maybe Belamae.

"Put in with the Reconciliationists," Ollie added, conversationally. "Best acquisition those religionists have had in some time. I imagine they weep when he sings the Petitioner's Cycle over at Bastulen Cathedral. Shame."

Divad said nothing. He'd denied Alosol's several requests for admission to Descant. The man had Lieholan in him, all right. And Divad would have liked to take him in. But as important as talent was, being teachable mattered more. Alosol carried himself with a callow arrogance, the kind that smacked of someone who thinks he's got the world figured out.

"Speaking of religionists," Ollie said, running the towel over the bartop by habit, "listen to this. I was laying up some of that there wheat bitter in the cellar, keeps the temperature right, you see. But I'm running out of room down there. So I'm moving shelves, and I find a cellar door I hadn't noticed before. A closet. Inside, there are maybe eight crates sealed tight. Dust on 'em as thick as carpet. And what do I find inside?"

He waited on Divad to guess.

"More bitter?"

"You lack imagination," Ollie quipped, proceeding with his discovery. "No, hymnals. And some other papers, besides. Turns out, before this place was Rafters, it was a chantry. Don't you just love that?"

Divad smiled over the top of his glass. He did, in fact, love that. The idea that these walls had been a devotional songhouse of sorts, even before becoming a tavern, tickled him for no good reason.

"To a new kind of sacrament, then," Divad said, hoisting his bitter. And part of him meant it. Songs sung in memoriam were damn important. Suffering itself took that theme more than once.

Ollie didn't drink. He tasted all his stock, but he never finished anything. 'I'll keep my wits, thanks,' he was fond of saying. But he took his bar rag and pretended to clink glasses with Divad.

"That's not the half of it," he went on, gleefully. "That stage, the balcony balustrade . . . my dear absent gods, even this bar," he chuckled, "altar and pews, all of it."

Divad drank down half his glass and nodded his amusement. Just then, the first musician of the night began. Divad swiveled in his seat to find a young woman slouching at the rear of the stage. Her first notes were hesitant, like a child stuttering. The melody—a mum's lullaby known as "Be Safe and Home Again"—hardly carried past the first table.

The first musicians of the night were those Ollie thought had talent, but who had little reputation yet. They played mostly to empty seats.

Beneath her timid first notes, though, Divad heard what Ollie surely had. He got the young girl's attention with a simple hand wave. When she looked over, he straightened up tall on his barstool, threw out his chest, tilted back his chin, and took an exaggerated breath to fill his lungs. He then narrowed his eyes, and screwed onto his face a look of confidence. The young girl nodded subtly, mid-phrase, and at her next natural pause, drew a deep breath, stepped forward on the stage, and threw back her head and shoulders. The diffidence of her tone vanished. A clear, bright sound transformed what had been a plaintively beautiful lullaby into a clarion anthem of hope.

Now that's teachable.

The rest of the night only got better. As music flowed from one to the next, Rafter's filled to standing room only.

Between acts, conversation buzzed with anticipation for the next performer. Divad would turn back toward the bar to try and avoid too many inquiries about Descant admission. Mostly that failed. But he did it anyway.

During one of the brief intermissions, an overeager percussionist sidled up close to him. To announce himself, he began to beat on the surface of the bar. With one hand he set a beat in four-four, while with the other he tapped increasingly faster polyrhythms: three-four, five-four, six-four, seven-four. He then repeated the entire cycle at double the tempo. It was rather impressive, actually. But when the young man reached out a hand in greeting, he knocked over Divad's third glass of wheat bitter. The amber liquid washed over the bar, giving the worn lacquer new shine.

Ollie appeared out of nowhere with his rag, and began mopping up the spill. Some of the bitter remained in shallow grooves scored into the bar.

The indentations looked familiar somehow, and Divad sat staring, thoughts coalescing in his mind. All kinds of songs had passed across this bar, ribald tunes, laments, fight and love songs (which he thought shared more in common than most other types), dirges. And those melodies had risen from strings and woodwinds and horns and countless voices.

And all that just since it had become Rafters. What about its years before that? Divad found himself grinning at the idea of countless songs for the dead sung here when it had been a chantry.

35

It got him thinking about sonorant residue—the idea that exposure to music could create subtle changes in the fabric of physical reality. The notion found its roots in the Alkai philosophies of music. To Divad's ear, the evidence was something you could hear in old, well-used instruments, and in the music of musicians who'd spent their lives listening, teaching, performing. *It got in you,* as was said. Not an elegant way to express it, but it got the point across.

Ollie had nearly finished drying the bar, when Divad caught his rag-hand. He tapped the bar. "What's this made of, my friend?"

Ollie's brow furrowed. He then produced a paring knife from his apron, bent down behind the bar, and a moment later stood up. In his fingers he held a thick curl of wood, presumably carved from the underside of the bar. He handed it to Divad, while continuing to stare at it with newfound interest.

Divad turned the shaving over in his fingers twice, inspecting the grain. He gave Ollie a quick glance, then put the curl of wood to his nose and breathed in deeply. He knew that scent like he knew the sound of his own voice. He turned his attention back to Ollie, grinning widely in spite of himself.

"I have a proposition for you, my friend."

Four

ISHIVERED, AND sweat dripped from my nose. I sat alone in a tent, huddled under three layers of rough wool blankets. The fire in the middle of the space leapt higher than was probably safe, but I kept adding more wood. I couldn't seem to get warm. The cold emanated from somewhere inside me. It felt as if I'd drunk a pitcher of iced water too fast, and was now experiencing the chill of it in the pit of my stomach. I'd downed several mugs of hot tea that hadn't helped a jot.

There wasn't really any mystery in it, either. I'd tried to repurpose Suffering. It had been an arrogant thing to do. And I was feeling the effects. The worst of it might be that I hadn't done much good. A few moments of song, a few dead Sellari, and then they'd carried me back from the line. It was embarrassing, really. They'd sent for me at Descant, like some bright hope. And I'd managed only a few passages of song for them.

I was able to let the failure go, though. Selfish to worry about my failing. I needed to figure out what I'd done wrong.

Suffering had nine passages:

Quietus

The Bourne

The Placing

Inveterae

War

Self-Destruction

Vengeance

Quiet Song

Reclamation

My first thought was that I'd chosen the wrong passage to sing. Aligning the right song to the right singer for the right encounter had been a Tilatian art of war since they'd escaped the Bourne. Perhaps I should have asked Baylet to assign me one of the songs I'd reviewed last evening.

But I quickly let go of that argument. I'd sensed that War had been the right air. In truth, there might be many *right* songs for any one moment on the line. Much of the choice of song had to do with the confidence a Lieholan had in the music. That hadn't been the problem for me, though. Something else, then.

Maybe it's as simple as the fact that I've never sung with this intention before.

That made sense. But it was also a depressing thought. It could mean I'd be no use to Baylet or our people. Or it could mean I'd wreak no vengeance for my da. The very thought of it brought a new wave of shivers. And in shivering, I happened on a new, entirely unpleasant idea. Maybe in turning Suffering into a song to suit my own need, a need to harm, I'd opened up a darker part of myself. An untested part. Like an unused muscle that, when overworked, tires quickly, making a man sweat and retch.

Could also be that the rough-throat technique itself had been my failing. Twice as hard as pure vocalization if it's done correctly. But I'd thought it would be second nature to me. Besides toying with it now and again back at Descant, I'd grown up hearing it a fair bit.

Whatever the reason, I'd failed to make Suffering the right kind of song to take to battle. And as I sat shivering, what worried me most of all was that I just wasn't cut out for this. I took another sip of strong sage tea, and was bending nearer the fire when Baylet ducked into my tent.

"Not a good day," he said right off.

I swallowed my tea and said nothing.

He sat across the fire from me, knitting his hands together. The scar on his neck caught the firelight in flickers of orange and shadow. "What did you sing?"

"Something from Suffering," I replied, looking down into my mug. "I thought the power of it would transfer . . ."

"Suffering?! Dear Lords of Song, you're crazier than your father." There was a soft chuckle. "I'm going to assume your Maesteri wouldn't approve."

"He might laugh, given how well it went." I wiped the sweat off my face. "And you might wind up disappointed you brought me here."

Baylet stared at me through the flames. "I already told you. I brought you back as much for you as I did for me."

"Ah, right. For my da. I imagine he'd be proud, too," I said with no small measure of sarcasm.

"You have a gift, Belamae, no question about that. But so do a hundred others just like you. I've no delusion that one voice will tip the scales in our favor. And you letting your failure color your sense of your father's pride is foolish. It's not honest either." He paused a long moment. "You probably failed because you're still looking at things for what they are."

"And what are they?" I asked.

Baylet pinned me with a thoughtful stare. But he never answered my question. The silence that stretched between us became uncomfortable. I shivered the whole time, inching closer to the fire so that my knees had grown hot.

Finally, he broke the silence. "Why Suffering? Was that your plan the whole time?"

I took up a stick and poked at the fire, causing sparks to be scattered up in the heat. "I think it probably was. Not the specific passage. But it's the one music none of the rest here know." I pointed vaguely toward the staging area with my stick. "And Suffering . . . there's a lot about it that makes sense here."

Baylet listened, never looking away from me. "And yet you told me your training wasn't complete. What do you know about absolute sound, then?"

The question didn't seem conversational. He was asking for a reason, and it had to do with more than just today's disappointment.

"A little," I answered. "Maesteri Divad tried to show me before I left. But I wasn't terribly receptive."

As I said it, I began to wonder if Divad had been coaching me, preparing me, for when I arrived here. Surely he'd known I wouldn't stay in Recityv. He could judge a stranger's intention from body language and the first word out his mouth. And he'd known *me* for four years.

"Absolute sound is the last principle of music you must master before you can sing Suffering the way it was intended." Baylet's eyes grew distant, staring across the flames. "And at their core, the Mor Refrains are written with the same principle in mind. There's more to them than that, but you can think of them in that way." His eyes focused on me. "Which is why we didn't bring them with us; why we never do."

I fought to remember what Maesteri Divad had said the last time we'd spoken, argued. Anything to help me pull myself from the music illness that had gotten inside me.

"And I still stand by that," Baylet said, though his voice didn't sound convincing. "But you . . . I need to tell you something. Things have changed during your four days—"

"Four days. What are you talking about?"

Baylet gave a weak smile with one corner of his mouth. "You slept straight through the first three. While you did, the Sellari changed their strategy." His eyes then widened with new understanding. "It makes sense now. They must have realized you'd sung Suffering."

"What makes sense?" I threw back my blankets, worry getting the better of me.

"All the Sellari coming at us now, on all fronts, are like our own Shoarden men. Our songs don't stop them." He scrubbed the stubble on his cheeks. "They don't hear us. We are reduced to steel alone . . . And we're outmanned five to one."

I felt a heavy pressure in my chest. "It's my fault," I muttered. "For trying to sing Suffering."

Baylet stood. "Timing is a hell of a thing, Belamae. If you'd had more training at Descant, the Sellari wouldn't need to hear your song for it to beat them down." He laughed bitterly. "That's not a fair thing for me to say. The use of song that way is precisely why the Mor Nation Refrains are held safe. Never sung."

Baylet then pulled a sword from beneath his own cloak and laid it on the ground. He stared at it for a moment before standing and leaving, not saying another word.

I sat listening to the crackle of fire, and watching the dull gleam of orange flame on the hilt of the blade. If I was no good with Suffering, I was utterly inept with a sword. In fairness, I hadn't spent any real time cultivating a feel for one. It would be as foreign to me as playing a new instrument.

Like a viola.

New shivers claimed me before I managed to crawl my way to my travel bag. Inside, I found the hollow oak tube I'd carried with me from Recityv. I pulled off the fitted plug on one end and gently removed the score Maesteri Divad had given me the last time we met. I carefully unrolled it, and scanned the music staff.

Scordatura.

Of course it would be this kind of notation for the viola d'amore. As I pored over the melody, I began to realize why Divad had given it to me.

I read and reread it for hours, and jumped when my tent flap was pushed back. Baylet poked his head inside. "The Sellari are pressing their advantage."

His eyes found the sword where he'd laid it down. I ignored the invitation and shrugged out of my blankets entirely. I stood, felt a bit woozy, but forced myself to follow him into the dark hours of night. As we went, I kept hearing the song my Maesteri had given me.

Scordatura. *Mistuned.*

FIVE

BEYOND THE WINDOW of Divad's lutherie, heavy rain fell, causing a distant hum of white noise. Now and then a gust of wind pushed drops against the glass, adding a plinky *tep, tep* rhythm to the music of the storm. It was late, well past dark hour, as he sat smoothing the piece of old spruce. He moved the rough horsetail back and forth with the grain, adding another rhythm to the music of the rain.

As much as he liked the still, warm moments of morning in his luthier rooms, nighttime, when Descant slept, could be just as enjoyable. And the sound of hand tools applied to wood to shape and refine, simple as it seemed, put him at peace. Perhaps molding an instrument that did not ask questions (as Lieholan incessantly did) had a certain appeal.

Whatever the reason, working with his hands felt good. It reminded him that he lived a unique life, a privileged life. It also reminded him that it had not always been so.

He finished smoothing the piece of Ollie's bar that would become the viola's top, and removed it from his bench dog and vise. Using a rasp, he filed the edges to conform perfectly with his original trace, and set to purfling the piece with a thin border. He finished that up, and added more oil to his lamp before setting to the most important part of reproducing the viola soundboard.

Before beginning, he took a deep breath of the spruce-and-maple scent that lingered in the air. This, too, he loved. The smell had a settling effect. Then he bent over the original instrument, which he'd carefully pieced back together with some hide glue. It would never hold together over time, but it gave him a good sense of what the top had looked like before Belamae shattered it.

He ran his hands carefully, lovingly, over every fraction of it, lingering on the original imperfections it had received here and there. Marks, dents, scrapes. He felt these for depth, length, ridges. He needed to understand them entirely.

He repeated the whole process twice more, then placed the new, smooth top back into his bench dog and vise. He picked up a fine-tipped taper punch with a rounded end. Methodically, working from the tail of the original instrument forward, he found the first mar in the wood, ran his fingers over it several more times. Then he turned his attention to the new wood. He'd never found wood inflexible or difficult to work with. For him it was as potter's clay. Just holding it gave him comfort. Particularly if that wood was on its way to becoming an instrument of some kind. Especially then.

When he felt ready, he began to score the new spruce top in the same place, and to the same depth and form as the broken viola. He worked slowly, applying a little pressure, compared the new mark to the old, then applied more pressure. He repeated this process until they seemed to him identical. Then he found the next imperfection, and worked that one.

He wanted everything as close to the original as possible, because he knew that all things affected the sound an instrument made.

The soundboard would vibrate when played. It transferred more sound than the strings alone. That was its whole purpose. It was key to the tonality of the instrument. And it all began with the wood itself. Spruce was stiff and light, growing slowly in alpine climes. It produced a lovely timbre. The age of the wood mattered. The manner of that aging mattered. The thickness of the soundboard also mattered. The walnut oil, as well. For Divad, there was also sonorant residue—the songs the wood had already *heard*. It was like a good chili. You never finished making it. You simply kept adding beans and peppers and corn and loin cuts. And the richness of the blend deepened as days went by. Good chili pots were never empty.

And past all that, an instrument received its share of wounds. Sometimes they were the result of careless hands, dropping something on the instrument or mishandling it in some way. Other times, the anger of a musician would have him lashing out. This almost always came from impatience with his own facility or technique. Still, it was often taken out on the instrument. More wounds. And then, of course, time takes its own toll. The smallest imperfection in the wood or the luthier's assembly of the instrument would result in changes that affect its sound, if only in the smallest degree.

And with more time, all those practically inaudible changes would accrete to something audible, giving each instrument its own voice, a rich blend of resonances that could never be duplicated.

Divad meant to reproduce *this* viola in as much detail as humanly possible. To get back its voice. It mattered. And later into the night, when he fingered a long deep scar in the original instrument's wood, he began to remember why.

With one hand holding forward her cowl, his sister, Jemma, held something out to him. "Take it," she said.

They stood on the west side of Descant in the shade of mid-evening. A pleasant after-rain freshness filled the air.

"What is it?" Divad asked, knowing very well what she proffered. He'd been at Descant only a year, but in that year his life had gotten busy. He hadn't been home in months. Whenever she came, her gift was the same.

Into his hand, Jemma dropped a pomegranate, its skin dry and pocked. Around it a note had been wrapped after the fashion of his father, who sold damaged fruit on the edge of the merchant district, where street carts were permitted. His and

Jemma's gifts on their name days and any other special occasion had been the same—father's best piece of fruit with a handnote as wrapping.

"Will you visit soon?" Jemma now used both hands to keep her cowl carefully in place.

Divad opened the note, which basically asked the same question, along with words of fatherly pride over Divad's being one of the select few admitted to Descant.

"I'll try," he said. "You don't know what it's like, though. There's so much to learn. Any time away puts me behind."

Jemma nodded inside her cowl. "Mother misses your laughter after supper. Especially since the harvest came in light."

That caught Divad's attention, if only for a moment. "Father's still selling what the merchant houses won't though, right? The older produce. The houses haven't taken that business back in, have they?"

"No," she replied, "but they may as well. There's not much left by the time it reaches father's carts. And what of it there is, he has to sell at less than half, it's so picked over."

"And you? You're well?" he asked.

She simply stared ahead. She stepped toward him and gave him a light hug with one arm, then turned to go. He said goodbye, and caught a brief glimpse of her face in the light of a clothier shop as she stepped past him. He should have stopped her to ask about the discoloration—or was it a shadow?— but she gave him little time and he was eager to get back to his study. If the pomegranate wasn't completely desiccated, it *would make a fine treat to accompany the memorization of the mixolydian mode.*

Divad's fingers began to tremble with the memory. He put the taper punch down, flexed his hands several times, then shook them to get the blood flowing. He sat back and drew several deep breaths. While waiting for his tool-hand to feel normal again after so long pinching the iron, he reached out with this other hand and again traced the scar in the viola's face.

It had gone much deeper than simply marring the lacquer. This gouge had gotten into the wood, and had torn along the soundboard for the length of two thumbs. It was by far the viola's worst scar. *Before Belamae shattered it.* His student might have been the one who slammed the instrument down, but Divad felt responsible. Just as he was responsible for this older scar in the viola face.

Divad looked away to the window, allowing the sound of the rain beyond to fill him. But try as he might to avoid it, the memory of the next time he saw Jemma rose like a specter in his mind.

The Cathedral quarter had once been the high district in Recityv. Now, it was maybe a hair's breadth better than a slum. The smells of bay rum sold by the cask, old urine-soaked straw and rotting mud, and unwashed day laborers filled the air. Jangly music drifted from the windows and open doorways of performance taverns. And children too young to be on their own either panhandled or waited with cunning eyes to pick the pockets of the unsuspecting.

Divad, oblivious to it all tonight, made his way through the streets to a familiar tavern. He needed a glass of wheat bitter to sip while he continued to struggle with the notion of attunement—a concept introduced to him that afternoon during a lecture on acoustics.

As he ambled toward the back corner, he passed a seated woman who kept her eyes lowered. At the edge of her table rested an empty mug. He'd nearly passed her when he realized who she was, and stopped abruptly.

"Jemma? What are you doing here?"

His sister's eyes flicked up to him with a mix of concern and embarrassment. She regained her composure within the time of a single breath. "Same as you, I would guess. Resting. Trying to shake off some of the street. Thinking."

He smiled and sat down opposite her.

"At home, it was strong tea and the stump behind the house." She returned his smile.

"Here it's wheat bitter and the stool in the corner," he said. "What about you? What are you drinking?" He pointed to her empty mug.

"Nothing. I'm fine," she replied rather quickly.

Divad nodded, recognizing when not to press too hard. "How's Father? Mother? Has the market gotten any better?"

When she met his eyes he noticed the same discoloration he remembered seeing . . . was that a year ago? But hadn't it been on the other side of her face?

"Father's selling road fare beyond the city wall now. The merchant houses haven't had fruit for him to vend in months."

A heavyset man with a ponderous belly that rolled over his belt like a water bag sauntered up to their table. "You going to buy the lady a drink? Or talk to her all night?"

"This is my brother," Jemma said evenly, without looking up.

Divad caught a twinkle of delight in the man's eye. "It's like that then. Well, I—"

"Go away," Jemma said flatly.

She sighed and pulled her empty mug back toward her. The heavy man huffed something under his breath and trundled away. Once he was gone, Divad ordered a glass of Kuren wheat bitter and set to explaining about acoustic attunement, and the parts he was struggling to understand. All the while Jemma nodded and smiled patiently. And though she seemed quite weary, she listened and asked questions. Later, they spoke of small things as only a brother and sister can.

Divad couldn't recall what, beyond attunement, he'd jabbered about that night with Jemma. The details were lost to him. But he remembered how it had felt to slip back into that unself-conscious kind of chat that didn't have to be about anything. Just talk for its own sake.

It had felt rather like the rain tonight. Soft, lulling. And yet, his hands continued to shake. It was the memory itself that unsettled him. A memory marked by this scar in the wood. To try and settle his nerves, he began to hum. He recalled a particular tune Jemma had been fond of. Then he picked up the taper punch again, holding it firmly but not too tightly.

Before he could begin, he heard the sound of steps behind him in the shop. "Maesteri?"

Divad remained poised, irritated yet also grateful for the intrusion. "Back here."

A third year Lyren stepped into the light of his lamps. There was a long moment, while Sedri, a woman gifted with a powerful alto voice, surveyed the tabletop. "Are you gouging a new soundboard?"

He let out a sigh, realizing she wouldn't be simply shooed away. Sedri was nigh onto fifty, coming to Descant after decades in the performance taverns. Despite her age, she could be as trusting as a child. But her many years had made her rather fearless, an important quality for someone doing the kind of singing he'd been teaching her.

He nodded for her to sit beside him. Then he gathered in her inquisitive stare, her original need of him apparently forgotten. "If you could go back," he began, fixing an instructive metaphor in his mind, "if you could back and do it again, would you spend those thirty years singing in smoke-filled taverns?"

She never averted her eyes, which, far from being sleepy at this forsaken hour, burned with the shrewdness of age. "You mean would I trade the smoke that has gotten into my vocal timbre."

Divad nodded. "You came by your craft a hard way. And those long nights airing out your songs through tabaccom haze has surely damaged your vocal chords. Given you some lovely alto tones, to be sure, but mostly given you a smoky sound."

She gave him a questioning look.

"That's not criticism," he added. "Your control and vocal strength are equal to or better than Lyren half your age. But . . ." he trailed off, forming his question more accurately, "if you could have the same facility in your voice, but have back the clarity, would you take it?"

After a moment, her face bloomed into a thoughtful smile. "No. I earned this tone."

He put a hand on her shoulder. "Just so. For my viola here, I'm doing my damnedest to be sure she has all the smoke and haze in her voice that she had before she was broken. Now, you get some sleep. You've a lesson on vocal dynamics tomorrow, and the regimen is an athletic one."

Sedri stood up.

"By the way, what was it you wanted when you came in?" Divad asked.

She smiled down at him. "I had a question about attunement. But I think I'll hold onto it for now."

When her footsteps had completely receded, Divad turned back to the new soundboard—his hands steady as wrought iron—and continued to scar the viola.

The smell of pine resin was strong in his parents' home. His father took in a plug every cycle for hauling away the carpenter scraps, which they'd always burned in their fireplace. The scent might have been a perfect welcome if Divad hadn't returned for Jemma's wake.

Six mourners—three of them unfamiliar to him—sat with his father and mother in the foreroom of their home. On the floor in front of the hearth lay a simple casket. The wood shape held an awful finality. Seeing it, Divad gasped. He hadn't been home in four years. Hadn't seen Jemma in . . . was it a year? More?

Time got away from him while he was concentrating on his studies. And until now, he'd given little thought to what he'd left behind.

He put down the viola case he carried, and went to his father. He struggled to find the right words. Really, his best response to this would be found in his music. He settled on, "I'm sorry." The words were entirely too small for the feeling inside him, inside this room. His mother reached up, still holding a kerchief, and grasped his wrist. Tortured eyes pleaded with him to do something.

"Oh Divad . . ." Her voice quavered. "We had no idea. We thought she took a laundry job. Her few coins . . ." She couldn't continue.

He looked at his father. "What happened to Jemma?"

The shame Divad saw rise on his father's face was terrible to see. Such a look of helpless failure. The man's own skin looked heavy on his bones.

His father softly cleared his throat. "Jemma took to beds to earn coin, Divad. The kind of man that would pay her . . . liked to use his fists. It's my fault, son. I should have been able . . ."

Divad began to feel a cascade of grief overwhelming him. Grief for Jemma; for his mother's broken heart; for his father's feelings of shame and failure; for his own absence during it all. He looked down at the top of the casket. Pine.

Before he realized what he was doing, he retreated to his instrument, unclasped the case, drew out the viola, and began to play without bothering to resin his bow or tune. He escaped into the only song that came to mind, "If I'm Reminded."

The sweet sound of his viola filled the room. It held the unique qualities of both eulogy and sympathy. Long mournful notes resonated beneath his fingers as he played for Jemma. As he did, the story of her life fell into place: the discoloration in her face when she'd handed him a pomegranate; his father's loss of his cart-trade; an empty mug at the edge of a table—a signal he hadn't understood until now; Jemma's lack of beauty, and the only kind of man willing to pay her—one who sought to brutalize as part of pleasure-taking.

He should have seen it before. He shouldn't have been so absorbed in his music that he failed to see or help. He began to hate himself for blathering on about his lessons while she *waited on the prospect of a few plugs in exchange for being beaten while giving up her maiden box.*

His music had gotten in the way. And yet even now he used it to find refuge from a pine overcoat and the anguish of people he loved but had rarely seen in four years. Refuge from his own shame.

Sometime during the chorus of his song, his grip loosened. His bow and viola slipped from his hands and fell, crashing against the wood scuttle.

Divad's hands became still. His left forefinger had come to the end of the original scar. His right hand remained poised with the taper punch near the surface of the new sound-board. The mark was complete; as nearly identical as he could make it. The one gouge in the antique instrument that utterly belonged to him.

His leaving for Descant to study music had meant one less wage earner to support the family. He couldn't have known the produce trade would wane, any more than he could have imagined his sister would take to the mattress to help earn coin. Jemma had never said a word. Not to him, and not to his parents. Her modest contribution had helped them continue to survive.

"If only I had been there," he muttered to himself, "instead of here."

Music, even the learning of music, had begun to mean something different after that. He no longer took it for granted. And he did his damnedest to put it after his family in his list of priorities. That had meant late-hour repair for fiddle players and the like, who were willing to pay a Maesteri to fix up their decrepit instruments. He'd started to become accustomed to the wee hours sitting in this very shop. And every plug or jot he earned made its way to his father, no matter how healthy the cart-trade was at the time.

As the rain continued to whisper beyond the window, he nodded to himself. The soundboard was done. But he didn't, just yet, stand to leave. Instead, he remained in the company of wood smells and old spruce, thinking about smokiness.

SIX

THE SELLARI PRISONER sat bound to the trunk of a tall poplar tree. I'd asked Baylet for a deaf one, like our Shoarden men. He'd assured me this one could not hear. The man appeared to have been severely beaten—for information, I assumed. The blood on his face had dried in the cold night air, and his chin hung slack so that his sleeping breath gave out slow tendrils of steam in the moonlight.

I stood a ways off, considering what I must do.

The lesson in the score given me by Divad had become clear. Scordatura was a kind of music notation used for altered tunings, as the viola d'amore usually had. That particular instrument was rarely tuned in fifths. In fact, it might employ twenty or more different tunings, each one to suit the individual piece. The various tunings made it possible to play chords and individual notes that weren't playable using conventional tuning.

Scordatura told the musician how to tune his instrument and where to put his fingers. But *not* what note to expect.

Some called it finger notation. On the page, the music appeared to be dissonant, filled with minor seconds. But because the strings were tuned differently, scordatura notation merely indicated finger position, the possible note combinations were unique.

That night I realized what scordatura could teach me about absolute sound, song with absolute value. That's why Divad had given me this piece of music in the Chamber of Absolutes. Trying to make sense of the notes proved frustrating, until I let myself simply consider where my fingers would rest on the strings, not knowing which note would sound, but trusting that the right one would.

Like scordatura tuning, singing a note with absolute value meant finding the right *place* inside a thing to resonate with, regardless of the note. If I meant to produce music that could stop Shoarden men, it would have to be of the absolute kind. I needed to figure out how to resonate with some part of them even when they could not hear me. I needed to go beyond my training, and figure out *where* to play these Sellari, the song of them.

In a real way, I'd be playing them like a scordatura-tuned viola d'amore. And the song that came out of me would resonate inside them as though they were aliquot strings.

I gave a weak but grateful smile, thinking of Maesteri Divad. He'd been trying to help me, even as he'd tried to convince me to stay. Perhaps he'd known I would come here to fight, regardless. But I still had to find that Sellari string to play. And looking back at the captive, I decided how I would do it.

As I approached him, the frozen ground crunched beneath my feet, the sound of it loud in the night. The Sellari couldn't hear me, so I tossed a small stone at his chest. His slack mouth slowly closed, and his eyes opened. He looked up at me, seeming to gauge whether or not he'd be beaten again. After a moment of silent regard, I allowed myself to become attuned to the figure sitting before me. To hear the song of him.

I began by focusing on his wounds, understanding how physical pain would feel in my own face and neck. Then I recalled the feeling of being restrained and threatened—a particularly worrisome moment I had suffered at the hands of a gang of five street brawlers the year I arrived at Descant. Then I summoned the images of the fallen from this very war, both theirs and ours.

Like a string being drawn across by a long bow, I began to feel the first notes of resonance between us.

In my mind, I identified musical phrases, performing mental turns in a descending Lydian scale to suggest surrender and helplessness and the simplest fear for self. And I let the look in the other's eyes, the vaguest hope of returning to his own loved ones, sweeten a bitter musical signature that rumbled inside me.

It wasn't the memories or thoughts themselves that brought us together, but their residue. The combinations of like things produced a kind of vibration we both shared.

I was attuned. I could hear the song of him. But what I had never done, never been taught to do, was sing that absolute value. Though now, I had a model for it. A scordatura model.

Rather than define the note or song I might sing to find a resonance inside him, I concentrated on a sense of him, the emotional fabric that made him who he was. And when that crystallized in my own mind, I opened my mouth and let come whatever most resonated with that sense.

I had never before made or even heard the sound that followed. It began as a low pitch that shifted so subtly that it lived in the space between notes. In those first few moments, the Sellari's ravaged lips curled into a smug smile; he must have thought he was safe from my song. But mere moments later, his brow tightened, creasing into several deep ridges. Concern rose on his face, his eyes darting from my mouth to my eyes and back.

I modulated a fourth up, then another minor third, singing with a glottal tone like the muggy feel of air thickened with rain. As I did, the Sellari's lips began to tremble, and a single runnel of blood issued from his nose.

He shook his head in confusion and worry, and pulled at his bonds in panic. I then began a steady pulsing change in pitch, letting each new note come without forethought, landing in a modal set unlike anything I'd ever heard—part Aeolian, part Dorian. But never rushed, and never loud.

When the Sellari looked back at me, abandoning his effort to break his bonds, the fear was so palpable I could feel it.

This was the moment of resignation that precedes some final pain or gasp. But this Sellari's pain was less about the fear of not living another day, and more about what he left behind: days he would never spend in the company of a son and daughter; regret for failing to do something he wished he'd made time for; the forgiving smile of his wife.

I sang his absolute value, resonated with him at the most fundamental level, and caused a violence inside him that tore him apart. He appeared to try and scream, but he could only tremble and sweat and suffer as my song undid him.

Finally, in a darkly beautiful moment, the resonance was complete. That's when I stopped, and he collapsed. The sweat and blood that coated him steamed in the moonlight. I felt both triumphant and sick inside, my own sense of attunement fading. But in those moments of song, I had found the place of the Sellari, that fingering a Lieholan could use to target the song of an entire people.

It was a broad and bloody thought. And once I'd found it, I began to weep. It was not a song I should know. The moral weight of that knowledge stole my strength and turned my legs to water. I fell to the mulch of rotting poplar leaves and sat there, smelling their autumn brown and the scent of cold soil.

Seven

DIVAD TURNED THE length of Pemam wood slowly over the alcohol flame. He'd been at it for three painstaking hours. He carefully heated each thumb-length of the bow-stick over a small clay pot filled with sour-mash-soaked gauze. Using a strong wheat whiskey served a whimsical notion he couldn't explain. He was also of the opinion that the spent wheat alcohol infused the bow with the grace seen in an unharvested wheat field brushed by a slow wind. Then he put the heated section to the camber, bending it gently before placing it on the edge of the flat bench. With a caliper, he measured the distance from the benchtop to the upper edge of the bow. For best performance, the bow camber needed to follow a gently increasing arc.

He turned a fair hand as a bowmaker, and had made countless bows in his day. The viola bow, in particular, proved to be a favorite, though, as its three extra finger-lengths over its violin counterpart allowed for a greater-than-usual variety of breaks and spreads. He'd fit it with a wider ribbon of horse hair, too—two hundred fifty strands. But the gradations he worked through now were the thing. They needed to be precise so that the bow remained equally flexible from tip to handle.

He sight-checked his work with a wooden template, too, though he preferred the exact measurements he got with his caliper.

Lesser luthier shops rushed through bow construction. They missed this crucial bit. Divad liked to tell his impatient students that: *The viola, it is the bow.* His overemphasis on the need for precision in its construction would, he hoped, mean they'd take care in all parts of making an instrument. It was true, though, that a well-made bow had a marked effect on the timbre of the instrument. More than anything else, he thought it gave the player a better hand at legato. Easy, fluid transitions in a piece most pleased his ear, so he didn't mind spending extra time to craft a proper bow.

He was in the process of bending in the delicate center-most section when indelicate footsteps crossed the luthier shop threshold.

"You'd best have a powerful reason for charging in all clumsy-like," he grumped. "You know this is delicate work up here."

"I think you can take a rest," came an unfamiliar voice. There was a calm but commanding tone in it, as from one who feels sure he'll be obeyed.

Divad released the pressure on the camber and looked under his armpit to see three men from the League of Civility entering his workshop. They weren't bustling, really. But they might as well have been, compared to the easy manner he instructed Descant members to use when coming into this place. The League liked to say of themselves that they *served the common interest*. Their emblem of four interlocking hands, each clasping the wrist of the next in a quadrangle-like circle, seemed comically obvious. Though the modest chestnut brown of their cloaks did just as good a job of conveying *common* while also setting them apart in uniform fashion.

He put the bow down gently and turned, wiping his hands on a dry cloth dusted with talc. "How can I help you gentlemen?"

The lead man slowed up, beginning to walk the line of instruments hanging from pegs in various states of repair. He ran a finger across each as he passed, the motion one part intimidation and another part casual familiarity. Close behind the other two Leaguemen came three Lyren, their arms outstretched as if they'd been beseeching their guests to slow down. Divad held up a hand for them to relax.

"Just some questions. Nothing that has to become contentious." The Leagueman's lips showed the barest of grins.

"Sounds harmless," Divad replied. "Always glad to educate. Shall we go and have a seat. I can offer you some—"

"What is it you do here?" the man asked.

Divad looked around. "I should think it's somewhat obvious. I repair instruments."

The man offered a soft chuckle. "You've wit. Please answer the question you know I asked."

"Fair enough." Divad leaned back against his workbench. "I teach music. And for some—those who have the gift—I teach *intentional* music. Most likely you call these folks Lieholan. It's as good a name as any, I guess."

"And these Lieholan, their job is singing a song that you would have us believe keeps us safe from mythical races, yeah?"

"A rather cynical way to describe it." Divad again wiped his hands of the sweat that had begun to rise in his palms. "If I look ahead of your questions, I suppose I'd say that what we believe on that score is ours to believe. And it doesn't cause a wit of harm to the League, or the people for that matter. May even lend some hope to weary—"

"Ah, see, that's the arrogance I expected." The Leagueman crossed to a near bench—the one where the glued viola rested beside a mostly reconstructed new one.

The stranger's nearness to the instrument made Divad panicky. "Does the regent know you're here? Or is this less ... *official*?"

Something changed subtly in the man's face. And it surprised Divad. The Leagueman's demeanor actually became less guarded, less scrutinizing, as he began to run his fingers along the unfinished viola. "Let me start over," the man said. It was a masterful change in manner. One Divad would have fallen for if he hadn't been changing the tone of his own voice to color vocal performance for the better part of thirty years.

Divad played along. "I'd like that. I'll admit to being a mite weary. So, truly, how can I help you?"

"I think maybe there's too much mystery around what Descant does these days," the man said. His tone was almost apologetic, as though he were on a forced errand. "I've been asked to invite several of your singers of Suffering back to help explain it to us." He smiled magnanimously. "I'll tell you something else. I'll wager when it's done, we find ourselves more kin than kessel."

Divad kept from smiling. *Kessel* was an Ebonian word that meant 'separated,' but most folks used it to mean 'enemy.'

"I'll be glad to accompany—"

"Not you," the man said abruptly, then raised his hands as though to revise his own terseness. "That's not how I meant that. I'd imagine you have a good handle on your purpose. It's those you teach that we need to talk to."

Divad began to lose patience. "Is this a trial of some kind? Because if it is, I'll want a letter with the regent's seal."

The man's stare narrowed, though his grin did not falter. "No. Not yet. But mind you, a man might wonder about the person who frets over being invited to explain himself."

"No," Divad said flatly. "You have no authority to insist. And none of us is freely going with you. We can talk here, if you'd like. Beyond that, I'll have to ask you to leave."

The man's genial manner fell away entirely. He stood glaring at Divad with calculating eyes. Then he turned to look back at the unfinished viola. He picked it up in both hands with a delicate kind of grace. The room fell silent and taut with expectation.

"It's fine work," the man said. "My father was a fair hand with a knife. Though he used his skill to gut sea trout and coalfish, and mend nets and loose deck planks."

"Sounds like a decent fellow," Divad offered.

The Leagueman nodded. "He was. Up until I was nine," he replied cryptically. He then began to wave the viola by its neck, his agitation slightly more manic. "Your students. They're free to choose whether to go, yes?"

"Of course," Divad said, tracking the instrument worriedly as the Leagueman began to use it to point around the room.

"What about you," he said, jabbing the viola toward the Lyren near the doorway. "Nothing preventing you from leaving, is there?"

The Lyren shook their heads rather emphatically.

He turned back to Divad, being sure their eyes locked. Then he raised his arm, and began to swing the viola down toward the workbench. Divad felt that sinking feeling again. His first thought was a random one: that instrument bows were historically a weapon, and how he wished just now he had the former kind. On the heels of that thought, song welled up inside him. It had nearly burst forth when the Leagueman stopped his swing and rolled the viola onto the tabletop. It fell harshly but remained unbroken.

The room hung in a stunned silence at the Leagueman's forbearance. After a moment he stepped close to Divad, an obvious attempt at intimidation. The smell of rain-soaked wool was strong.

"You don't recognize me, do you," the Leagueman said, his voice deep and soft and accusatory.

Divad shook his head. "You have my apology if I should."

The man leaned in so that his lips were near his ear. Softly, he began to hum a chromatic scale. When he reached the upper end of his middle register, his voice broke over the passagio—the natural transition point in the vocal chord between middle and upper registers. It was a difficult transition to master. But absolutely necessary for advancement at Descant.

It wasn't the break that brought the man's name to mind, though. It was the timbre of his rich bass voice. "Malen."

He'd spoken the man's name without thinking, and drew back to look him in the eye. Years ago the young man had simply left Descant, after struggling for the larger part of a year to learn how to sing over the passagio.

"You needn't have left," Divad said, offering some consolation. "We'd have found a way."

Malen smiled bitterly. "And I'd have believed you. They all do." He reached down and picked up the bow Divad had been shaping. "Still using sour mash, I see."

"Let me pour you a drink. Settled nerves make better music."

"You and your music metaphors. A teaching technique, yeah? Well, Maesteri, you then are Descant's bow." He tapped the side of Divad's neck with the length of Pemam. "And you play each Lyren for the fiddle he is."

Divad felt some compassion for the man. Each musician hits several potential break points—passagios of a different kind—that they either work through or are defeated by. But Divad's sympathy quickly turned to anger. He didn't like being threatened. Less so here within the walls of Descant. And least of all in the peaceful confines of his lutherie. "Don't retaliate against us because you failed here. Or are *you* still being played, only the fiddler now is the League Ascendant?"

Malen brought the unfinished bow up between them, and began to slowly bend it, holding Divad's defiant gaze while he broke the Pemam stick in two. The two Lyren at the threshold gasped.

"Maesteri?" he said, "I'm not asking permission. Four of your Suffering singers will come with me. We have some questions we'd like answered. If we find everything here is aboveboard," he gestured around to mean Descant, "they'll be back soon enough. And because I'm fair-minded, I've left you two Lieholan to sing Suffering. Just in case I'm wrong that it is all myth."

He grinned and departed unceremoniously, leaving Divad breathless with anger. When Malen left the cathedral, Geola, Harnel, Pren, and Asa left with him.

It wasn't a quarter hour before another visitor came to Descant's doors. This time it was the young regent, in her seat less than a year. She explained that the League had twisted a new law, the Rule of Impartiality—meant to prevent treachery. Under its provisions they were broadly questioning various affiliations throughout Recityv. She'd heard they were coming here. And she apologized for arriving too late to help.

"What can I do?" Divad asked.

The young regent, Helaina was her name, answered, "Come with me."

He put out his alcohol flame, doused his lamps, and pulled on his cloak. He gave brief instruction to Luumen, the senior of the two remaining Lieholan to whom he was leaving Descant while he was away. Then he hastened into the street, and struggled to keep pace with the purposeful gait of his regent.

Anger and worry twisted in his gut. He caught her eye and asked, "Can they really do this?"

She gave him a reassuring wink. "Not while I'm around," she said, and if it was possible, strode faster still.

EIGHT

I NEVER MADE it to the line. After singing the Sellari to death, I crawled back to my horse, and eased my way to my tent. I'd found an absolute sound, and the weight of it proved difficult to bear. Some songs were heavy. Knowing them was like shouldering a yoke of brick. Suffering was that way. Suffering was an absolute song. Its passages swirled in my mind now that I better understood its underpinning.

Near dawn, Baylet slipped into my tent again. He sat beside the sword he'd given me, which remained untouched. After a long moment he spoke wearily. "We lost two thousand men tonight."

I'd have thought there'd be a tone of indictment in his voice. But really he was just tired. Tired in his body. Tired somewhere deeper.

As I sat with him, we both kept our own observances for the unspeakable loss. Sometime later, while he stared away southward, he said, "You killed the Sellari."

It wasn't something I wanted to talk about. I said nothing.

"You found a way to sing death to a Shoarden man. We need your help."

Phrases of Suffering began to repeat themselves in my head. "I'm not sure I can."

"Because you can't? Or because you won't?" If Baylet hadn't been so weary, there might have been some impatience or indignation in his tone. As it was, mostly the question rang of disappointment.

It's how my father might have sounded, were he here to ask me the same. But I wouldn't have had any better answer for him. The best response I had was to keep silent.

Baylet shut his eyes and pinched their inner corners as his face tightened in a moment of frustration. When he let go, he tapped the sword beside him as one who's accepting the way of things. But rather than leave me alone, he said, "While you work through your personal grief, do me one last favor."

I gave him an expectant look, preparing for a barrage of insults. Instead, he stood and ducked out through the tent flap. A bit reluctantly, I followed. To my surprise, he neither rushed nor led me south. At an almost leisurely pace, our horses walked north and a smidge east. Moment by moment, the world awakened, near to dawn as it was. Animals skittered in the underbrush, birds began to call against daybreak in that soft way that keeps morning peaceful.

Several leagues to the west, the tips of the Solden range showed the sunlight gradually working its way down the mountains as the sun rose in the east. Before it reached the valley, Baylet stopped. I came up beside him and looked out over a vast field riddled with humps of freshly dug earth. There might have been eight hundred that I could see. In the distance, the field sloped away from us.

"I told you before. We're losing the war." Baylet took a deep breath, one that sounded like acceptance.

The graves of soldiers, then, I imagined. Unmarked barrows of the thousands who had fallen. It was a grim thing to see.

"The histories tell of the Sellari. Of the devastation when they lay hold of a place or people." Baylet surveyed the field left to right before continuing. "Rough hands, Belamae. They've no interest in servitude. They're glad to make sport of the living before putting them down for good. That'll mean indignities for families before the blessing of death."

"We could retreat north—"

"And leave the Refrains for the taking, you mean."

I shrugged. "Sounds like that's going to happen sooner or later."

The field leader became reflective. "Maybe. But trying to move so many so fast . . . and the Sellari would follow. The feud is an old one. It goes beyond the Refrains."

I'd not heard of this, and Baylet didn't offer to explain. So I let it pass.

"Rough hands," he said again. "They're coming. I don't have anything to stop them." He surveyed the field from right to left this time. "They knew it. And they did not wait . . ."

That's when I realized what I was truly looking at. Not the graves of his men. But killing fields. All Mor nation children were taught a simple, dreadful lesson when they reached their twelfth name day. If invasion should come, and defeat appear inevitable, our people would not wait for cruel foreign hands to take our lives. By our own hands, we would go to our last sleep with quiet dignity.

"There are at least a dozen more killing fields." Baylet's tone was filled with self-loathing. "They've begun to lose hope. By every abandoning God, this is too much!"

The field leader's voice boomed out over the field in long rolling echoes.

I wanted to say something. I wanted to say I would try. But my mind felt like an open wound that even a stir of wind would sear.

Baylet rode forward before I could find any words. I followed again, and soon we were navigating carefully between the graves. I noted the awful sight of patches of earth not much longer than the length of my arm. My mind conjured images of mothers offering their babes what they thought of as a mercy. If I'd felt disheartened before, if I'd thought I was too far from shore, now I felt lost and empty in a way only one song had ever taught me.

Before I could run that song through my mind, Baylet stopped and dismounted. I did the same. We stood together as the sunlight finally touched the field where we were. Our shadows fell across a pair of graves.

"I don't understand what it's like to sing an absolute," he began. His voice sounded strangely prayerful in that day's first light. "I've read the music of countless composers who've tried to write it down. Black scores. The kind whose melodies never go out of your head, though you wish they would." He shook his head slowly. "But they're just approximations. The ability to actually do it . . . it'd be a burden. A lot like keeping the Mor Refrains is a burden, I suppose. I'd like you to know, before I sent for you, my petition to the king for access to the Refrains was denied."

It seemed obvious now that all along Baylet had meant for me to find and sing the Sellari absolute. I felt duped. But I didn't have the energy for anger, and simply nodded.

Later, as the field began to warm in the sunlight, I asked, "Why are we here?"

He continued to stare down at the two graves. "Some by tincture. Others by rope. And more by blade drawn across blood veins."

Then it dawned on me. We must be standing over the barrows of his family. He fought for Y'Tilat Mor. He fought for his men. But after it all, he fought for those closest to him.

"I'm sorry," I offered.

For the first time, he looked up from the graves, giving me a look that passed from puzzlement to understanding to sympathy in a breath. "No, Belamae. We honor your mother and sister this morning."

My stomach tightened, and I felt instantly shaky. Baylet put a hand around my shoulders. Some faraway part of me thought again of how the field leader was orchestrating, influencing my decisions. But I'd have wanted to know. And no matter when or where, I'd have felt the same.

I drifted in a haze for I don't know how long, while grief pounded at my chest with its insistent rhythms. I couldn't keep from picturing ma and sa putting a knife to their own flesh. I felt their powerlessness and despair. And the dignity with which they went to their final earth, avoiding rough hands that—if things were left unchanged—would surely come.

Without realizing it, the words and melodies that had been circling in my mind started to come out. The sixth passage of the Song of Suffering: Self-Destruction, which was sung about the Inveterae condemned to the Bourne, countless of whom had taken their own lives rather than go to that awful place.

I sang the lament, gathering quiet strength with each phrase.

I lent it a measure of absolute value.

And I wondered if in so doing, somewhere ma and sa felt my song, though like Shoarden men, they would never hear it.

NINE

THE STREETS OF the Cathedral quarter were just beginning to come alive with the night arts. Confidence men sized up marks; sheet women angled for lonely men with spare coin; performance taverns were opening their windows, using music as a lure to drink and be entertained. More than a few packs of bearded men stood wearing hard looks, spoiling for fights. Through all this, Divad lead his four Lieholan.

For the better part of two straight days, he and Regent Helaina had argued with League leadership, clarifying the Rule of Impartiality, describing the workings of Descant Cathedral, growing angry. They'd had to involve the Court of Judicature, which helped but also delayed his students' release. By the time the League set them free, the thuggish treatment they'd received was visible on their faces in dark and purpled spots. They were exhausted, but alive.

Divad hadn't had time to put the ordeal into any kind of rational context yet. After a hot bath, warm meal, and night of uninterrupted sleep, he'd need to do that. They turned onto the quarter road that lead to the cathedral's main entrance. No sooner had they come in direct sight of Descant, than the door was opened and three Lyren began gesturing urgently for them to hurry.

He broke into a run, his cloak seeming suddenly over-large and cumbersome. Behind him, the slap of Lieholan shoes on paving stones followed close. He darted through crowds, around wagons and carriages and riders. He climbed the cathedral steps two at a time. One of the Lyren, Waalt, grabbed his arm and began to run with him, guiding him, pulling him along.

"What is it?" Divad asked, breathless.

"Luumen fell ill with autumn fever a day ago." Waalt pulled him faster.

Divad understood immediately. "How long?"

"Almost three entire cycles." Waalt's voice cracked with desperate worry.

"Dear merciful gods."

Luumen was the more experienced and stronger of the two Lieholan he'd left behind. Ill with fever, she would not have entered the Chamber of Anthems to sing Suffering. Which meant Amilee had been singing Suffering by herself.

"My last sky," Divad whispered, and pushed his legs to go faster.

It took nearly nine hours to sing Suffering's nine movements. After singing the cycle, the Lieholan was spent, and needed two days' rest to fully recover. There'd been occasions when one vocalist sang part of a second cycle. But it was rare, and always came at great personal cost to the singer. Amilee had been at it for not just two full turns, but nearly three . . .

Casting a look backward, he called commands. "Pren, prepare yourself." Pren's bruises were the worst, but he was also the strongest Lieholan Descant had since Belamae's departure. The young man stripped off his robe mid-stride, and began to run vocal scales as he maneuvered up beside Divad. "Asa, fetch a Levate." Divad didn't hold much hope that a physic healer could help, but he'd be prepared in any case.

The sound of their racing feet filled the cathedral halls. The flames of wall lamps fluttered with their passage. Lyren watched them go by with grave looks in their eyes.

Moments later, Divad pushed open the heavy oak doors to the Chamber of Anthems. Amilee was on her hands and knees, unable to hold her head up, singing toward the floor. Her voice sounded like corn husks brushed together by summer storm winds. She had almost no volume left. But the perfect acoustics of the rounded chamber lifted the delicate song she could still make, and gave Suffering life.

Pren picked up the melody line just a pace or two inside the door. When Amilee heard it, she did not look up at them, but simply ceased singing and collapsed on the stone floor.

Divad swept the girl up and carried her straight through the chamber and out the opposite door. He cut left to the nearest bedchamber and went in. He laid her gently on the coverlet, while Harnel fetched a pillow for her head.

Amilee's eyes fluttered open. "Maesteri," she said with a bruised voice.

"Save your words," he admonished. "Gods, I'm sorry, my girl."

He had to hold at bay renewed anger at the League, who had put them in this situation. His growing hatred for them would not help this courageous young woman.

She shook her head in a weak motion. "I didn't lag," she whispered.

Divad's pride in the girl swelled, tightening his throat with emotion. But he managed a low sweet tone, to course gently through her. Help him see, or rather, feel. So that even then, he knew she would not live. If her wound were of the flesh, he could render a song of well-being. But Suffering drew on a different part of a Lieholan's life. And of that, she had expended too much. It was remarkable that she had anything left. But it was not enough for him to resonate with.

Oh child.

As she lay dying, Divad found strength enough to put away his ill feelings for the League. He sat beside her and took her hand and sang a song of contentment. Slow and low, he poured out his love and admiration for the girl. He watched as the pain in her eyes and brow slowly relaxed.

And before she let go, he leaned in close, so that no one would hear the question he asked of her. When she nodded, she looked grateful and at peace.

Divad resumed his melody and sang until her hand grew cold. It was a dreadful thing to feel the song go out of a person for good. To feel the vacancy, the silence, that replaced what once was the resonance and melody of a life. His voice faltered more than once as he sang into the emptiness she left behind. He would have liked to play his viola for her, but it was still missing its strings.

TEN

FOUR DAYS AFTER Amilee went to her final earth, Divad sat again in the warmth and silence of morning sunlight inside his workshop. Motes danced slowly in the shafts of light, reminding him that even in silence there's a kind of song that stirs the air. These last few days he'd been preparing gut for his viola. Now, all that remained was to string the instrument.

Gut was best taken from the animal while the body is still warm. It needed to be stripped of fat and placed in cold water. Later, it would be transferred to wine or a solution of lye to help remove any last unwanted matter that still clung to it. Strips were cut to length, twisted together in various numbers to create different pitches, and rubbed with almond or olive oil to prevent them from becoming brittle.

Divad had thoughtfully done all this, and now picked up the first length and began stringing the repaired viola. One by one he fixed the aliquot strings to their bone points, and ran them up through the neck to their pegs. When he'd finished the resonant gut, he did likewise with the playable strings.

Next he tuned the instrument. Never rushing. Turning the peg as he thumbed each string to find the extended tuning for the first song he intended to play on the salvaged viola. The sounds of the tuning were somehow muted in the morning stillness, almost as if the air was resisting the sound.

When the instrument was finally ready, he sat back, regarding the fruits of his labor. The work had been tedious and filled with reminders. Both things were part of the process, something he knew from experience. But he felt satisfied that he had done well, and smiled genuinely for the first time in many days.

In every part, there'd been meaning. That mattered. From the spruce top harvested from a performance tavern bar, to the gut that Amilee had willingly surrendered from her own body. This last element might prove to be the most important, Divad thought. If there was truth to his notion of sonorant residue, then a piece of Lieholan that had sung Suffering might make this incarnation of the viola better than its predecessor. To teach resonance and play for the fallen, he could think of nothing better.

When the moment felt right, he took up the viola, and the bow he'd completed the prior day, and stood in the light of the window. There, he drew the bow across the gut, fingering the first notes of "If I'm Reminded." He then muted the top strings, and listened intently as the aliquots continued to resonate in the silence that followed.

A long time, he thought, and smiled. *A long time since I've heard this song.* Later, when the resonating strings ceased to hum, he would play it for Amilee. He'd play it finally for Jemma. For now, though, he stood still, allowing the aliquots to ring, and learning something more about resonance.

ELEVEN

IT WAS NOT DAWN when I arrived at the line. Midday had come and gone.

It was not the start of battle. They'd been fighting for hours.

It was not ceremonious. I simply found the front of the line and started to sing.

I sang the song of them. And almost without thinking, I blended the absolute value of the Sellari with a passage of Suffering—Vengeance.

Before my training at Descant, my experience with the word, even the *idea* of vengeance, came mostly from pageant wagon plays. Now I realized they'd treated the notion rather too simplistically. And I thought I understood why. Either the players didn't themselves really know. Or, if they knew, they believed most folks would be better off remaining ignorant on the topic. For that, I wouldn't blame them.

Then later, under the tutelage of the Maesteri, as I learned Suffering, my understanding of vengeance grew by half. But it was still a clean thing, theoretical. It remained a nearer cousin to the pageants, where vengeance sounded like melodrama, performed by a player wielding a wooden blade, wearing a silly mask, and moving in exaggerated motions. If it had a sound, it was that of a recalcitrant child screaming, "I'll get you back."

My Sellari song of vengeance was nothing like this. It was blind and messy. It pulsed with hatred. It knew nothing of justice or balance or *making something even*. And if my other recent songs had been rough-throat, this sounded as though I'd just gargled with crushed stone. I half expected my throat to start bleeding.

So I walked into their midst, unhurried, letting the song out. It was like playing a great chord, strumming a thousand strings. Ten thousand. Some men simply fell. Others began losing blood from every orifice. The flesh of many sloughed from the bone. Wails of anguish filled the air. There came the sound of countless bodies thumping onto cold ground. Some made a few retreating steps before the song got inside them.

Bright red blood spilled across the vast field.

It was a terrible song. And it was also mine. Since at his core it was resonance.

The property of resonance in sounding systems serves as a metaphor for love. One system can be set in motion by the vibrations of another. Two things, people or strings, trembling alike for one another.

That was one of the first Predicates of Resonance. The awful, practical knowledge I added to it was this: there were many resonances that could cause a man to tremble; love was but one of them.

With each note, my song grew stronger, feeding off itself, swelling as a wave traveling a broad ocean. I had no idea which of my enemies actually heard me sing, but it didn't really matter. Even if it wasn't heard, this song was felt.

When I finally stopped, I had no idea how long I'd been singing. It might have been a few long moments. It might have been hours. An eerie silence fell across the vast field. Not a single Sellari stood between my countrymen and the far tree line.

But there came no feeling of relief or triumph. The desire for vengeance still surged inside me. That's when I learned the hardest truth about vengeance: it had no logical end, served no real purpose, except perhaps to delay grief. Vengeance was just an inversion of loss; or maybe its cowardly cousin.

But it did have consequences.

Though I'd survived its singing, the song had done something to me. I knew it when the first Mor congratulated me. I didn't feel happy that this fellow would return to his family. Instead, I wondered and worried whether I'd saved a Mor who would bugger his son or beat his wife or ignore a daughter who only sought his approval. The cynicism ran deep, painful. It sickened me. And I instinctively knew that the only relief I'd find for this new pessimism was to continue singing the song.

Dear absent gods, give me someone to hate.

That prayer seemed to find an answer. Two hundred strides away, at the long tree line of poplar, hundreds of fresh Sellari emerged, striding purposefully toward us. In their midst, four Anglan draft horses pulled a broad flatbed wagon bearing a spherical object two strides in diameter.

I felt an eager smile creep onto my face, and I began to close the distance between myself and this new crop. To their credit, the second-wave Sellari came on bravely, as though they hadn't seen how I'd sung down those whose bodies I now trod on in my haste. I wanted to be closer this time. I wanted to watch them suffer as they went down.

Sea-crossing bastards killed my father. Forced ma and sa to . . . Inveterae filth, I will shatter the bones inside you. No, that is too good an end. I will find the point of resonance in your shank-given race and will make it your misery, show you the end of your women and children, their slow despair. I will break your hearts before tearing away your flesh.

With that, I rushed forward. I could hear the sound of running steps trying to keep pace with me—the Shoarden men assigned to keep me safe. But I cared none for that. When I was five solid strides from the Sellari, so that I could see the lines in their faces, I began to sing the shout-song again. I lent it a new intention, infusing it with the menace of hopelessness, like the sound of a screaming parent when she finds her child dead by her own hand. I knew such a sound from many years ago—that memory came back with a vengeance of its own.

I watched, eager to see the look in their eyes as they felt that deep ache before I broke their bodies.

But nothing happened. None paused or flinched or grimaced. They just kept coming on in the face of my song.

I was nearly upon them when I realized why.

This new brigade was dressed like Sellari, carried the same slender arcing sword. They'd even painted the same black band around their eyes. But they weren't Sellari. They strode with the swagger of mercenaries who lived for the opportunity to kill. Their grip and motion with their blades made it clearer still. They were not tense or overeager. A frightening casual readiness marked them. These were Holadai, fortune-swords. My Sellari song was useless against them.

More than that, each next note became more painful to sing. I tried to modulate the song, switch modalities, shift its intention, but nothing helped. And I watched in a kind of stupor as one of the Holadai reared back and threw a heavy hammer at me. I saw it come, and knew the aim was true. But stunned by the deception of this mercenary force, I couldn't move. The iron hammer hit me hard in the chest, where I felt ribs crack.

It knocked the wind from my lungs and drove me to my knees. Two pair of boots came into view, swords swinging casually. I saw them rise up out of my field of vision, and sensed they'd soon end my pain.

Then a flurry of footsteps rushed in around me. The clash of steel rang sharply against the sky. A Mor fell dead beside me, as did a Holadai. Then a spray of something warm and sticky caught me in the face. I fought to take a breath, but still could not. Around me more of my countrymen fell hard to the cold ground, as Holadai grunted and fought through their own wounds.

When at last I gasped a painful stuttering breath, I took in the coppery smell of blood. I grew blind with rage, and pushed myself to my feet. I fixed my eyes on this new enemy and summoned a different song. When I let it go, the air shivered with the harsh sound of it. The rasping noise tore at everything, shrieking through the minds and bodies of the Holadai.

As they began to drop, new forms took their place. My song caught in my throat to see that these replacements were a mix of Sellari and Holadai Shoarden. They wore menacing grins as they rushed toward me.

Fine trickery, you damned wharf-whores!

A stabbing pain fired in my thigh. I looked down to see an arrow protruding from my trousers. Around me, my Shoarden men were falling in alarming numbers. Frustration mounted inside me. I staggered backward a few paces. Another arrow caught me in the shoulder. This one I reached up and ripped out, feeling its barbs pull at my flesh.

The number of Sellari and Holadai became overwhelming. I didn't know how to help myself or my countrymen. But I had to do something. On instinct, I started to sing. *At the end of it, get the sound out,* I remembered Divad saying—the lesson an old one.

I began with a dire shout-song, a rough-throat cry I simply made up as I went. Then every third beat I switched, singing the song of the Sellari. I sang faster, the two songs beginning to come in a strange syncopation. And each time I changed, different men screamed, different bodies dropped.

I felt another hammer strike me. But it seemed somehow far away, and only hit me in the elbow—maybe breaking it, but that pain felt distant, too.

The real pain came each time I sang the notes of the Sellari song. The large sphere, now twenty strides away, amplified the music and reflected it back toward me. It didn't deflect the song from striking at the hearts of the Sellari. But it more than doubled the personal cost of the resonation I felt. The pain grew fast, much the way one's palm begins to burn when held close above a candle flame.

But I did not stop. The alternating songs wove in and out of one another, reminding me of waves rolling onto a shore and back.

Then, again, sometime later, all motion stopped. Heaps of bodies lay across the field, some stacked three deep around me. When I ceased to sing, silence returned to the world.

My face and hair, and all my clothes were drenched with blood.

I thought I heard the distant song of mockingbirds in the poplar trees. I couldn't be sure. My ears rang with the remnants of my own music. In those first moments of stillness, my cynicism, and the terrible ache that only singing destruction would assuage, began to plague me again. So once more, I wished for someone to hate. Looking far ahead, I saw several thousand Sellari stepping tentatively from the shadows. I started to smile. Then stopped.

Walking slowly toward me, across the bloodied field, came a line of Sellari women . . . and children.

At this new sight, I felt my mind break. That was the only way I could explain it.

Behind them strode fresh Sellari bladesmen and archers.

I watched them come, sensing an awful truth. This was not simply an invasion force. They'd come to occupy the Mor Nations, bringing with them their families, which they'd now turned into a walking shield.

A distant pluck and hum sounded, like a chorus of cellos being tuned. A moment later the sky darkened with arrows whistling toward us. Questions vied inside me. Could I let fly my own weapon, and sing the Sellari song into the bodies of the innocent? On the other hand, could I let them rain down death on my own people?

My struggle seemed endless, but in truth lasted only a moment. I felt my song rising, and hated myself for it.

Belamae?

The name came at me as though I stood at the bottom of a deep, dry well.

Belamae? It's over. Can you hear me?

I felt my body being shaken, but ignored it, my song touching my vocal chords, ready to be loosed.

Belamae? A sharp crack on my cheek stalled my song, and I was suddenly staring into Baylet's concerned eyes. "Are you all right?"

Confused, I slipped to one side, looking south to the line of poplar trees. Nothing. The field still lay quiet with thousands of the dead. But there were no archers. No women. No children.

"You found their song," Baylet said, his voice solemn.

I only nodded, slowly realizing that my mind had conjured a need to sing out Vengeance again. *Oh dear merciful music, what I was prepared to do.*

I fell to my knees and buried my face in my hands, weary, ashamed, relieved . . . changed. Song had become something I would never have imagined. A burden.

I also thought I finally understood what it would truly take to sing Suffering.

And I meant never to do it.

Twelve

WHEN THE DESCANT doors were pulled open, Divad looked out on an emaciated, disheveled figure. If he hadn't been told in advance, he might not have recognized Belamae. But it would not have been because his returning student looked as if he hadn't eaten in weeks or that his cloak was tattered and reeked of his unbathed, filthy body. Rather, his face was changed, his aspect. The useful intent in his eyes had gone away.

Everything about him gave Divad the feeling that he'd come here only because he didn't know where else to go. Belamae made no attempt to enter, or speak. He didn't even look up, simply staring downward, his hands hanging at his sides.

He looked too fragile to embrace, so Divad gestured him inside. The heavy doors closed with a deep, resounding boom. In the lamplight, he hummed a very low, very soft note. It was brief, but enough to resonate with the change that had gotten inside his prodigy. He gave a sad smile that the boy did not see, and turned, motioning Belamae to follow.

He walked slowly, without speaking, knowing that the soft resonant hum of Suffering that could be heard in the very stone of Descant would reacquaint the lad with the purpose of this place. That'd be a good start to righting his sense of things. The boy had a form of what the early Maesteri called *Luusten Mal.* Sound poisoning. It was a rather simplistic way of referring to it, but accurate in its own way.

Divad considered returning to the Chamber of Absolutes, where he'd first tried to impart a sense of absolute sound by way of aliquot strings and the viola d'amore. Instead, he turned down a different hall, and went up four levels by way of a spiral staircase, where the granite steps had been worn enough to resemble thin smiles.

Eventually, he led Belamae into his eastern-facing lutherie. He came to the worktable where he'd spent so many hours over these last many cycles, carefully repairing the instrument his student had destroyed.

He lingered a moment in the clean scent of spruce shavings made by recent work with a hand plane—he'd begun a mandola as a gift to a prospective Lyren he'd denied admission. But the viola was the reason for coming here. It rested on a three-legged stand very like an easel. He gently picked it up and turned toward the lad.

With slow deliberateness he stepped forward, watching as realization dawned in Belamae's face. He saw shame pass to surprise, to wonder, then to delight. That last came as little more than a faint smile, not unlike the surface of the stone steps they'd just climbed.

Relief held in his prodigy's eyes more than anything else, though. And he liked the look of that. It made every moment of remembrance and backaching work bent over his table worth the pain. But there was still an emptiness in the boy. He could feel it, like the reverberating resonance felt in the head of a tightly covered drum.

As he stared at Belamae, the right thing to do occurred to him. He extended the viola to him again, as he'd done what seemed like many cycles ago. Belamae tentatively reached for the instrument. But before his student could take it, Divad whipped it around and brought it crashing down on the hard oak surface of his worktable. The viola strings twanged, the spruce split and splintered, the body smashed into countless pieces, and the neck ripped in three parts. The soundboard he'd labored over lay in ruins. He felt a pinch of regret over it.

But his own loss was nothing compared to the shock and horror that rose on Belamae's face. It looked like the boy had been physically wounded. His mouth hung agape, his hands held out, palms up, as if beseeching an answer to the violent, incomprehensible vandalism.

"My boy," Divad said, his voice softly intoning some reason to all this. "Won't you help me collect the pieces. We'll see what's salvageable."

"Maesteri?"

Divad smiled warmly. "Instruments can be mended, Belamae." He tapped the lad's nose. "Come. We'll see about this together. I've decided I rather like this part of instrument care."

He began to hum a carefree tune, as they gathered in the shattered viola.

Read on for a preview of the

AUTHOR'S DEFINITIVE EDITION OF

THE UNREMEMBERED

BOOK ONE OF

THE VAULT OF HEAVEN

by

PETER ORULLIAN

THE
UNREMEMBERED

The Vault of Heaven

"One is forced to conclude that while the gods had the genius to create music, they didn't understand its power. There's a special providence in that, lads. It also ought to scare the last hell out of you."

—Taken from the rebuttal made by the philosopher
Lour Nail in the College of Philosophy
during the Succession of Arguments on Continuity

WHAT HADN'T BEEN BURNED, had been broken. Wood, stone . . . flesh. Palamon stood atop a small rise, surveying the wound that was a city. Beside him, Dossolum kept a god's silence. Black smoke rose in straight pillars, its slow ascent unhindered by wind. None had been left alive. None. This wasn't blind, angry retaliation. This was annihilation. This was breakage of a deeper kind than wood or stone or flesh. This was breakage of the spirit.

Ours . . . and theirs, Palamon thought. He shook his head with regret. "The Veil isn't holding those you sent into the Bourne."

Dossolum looked away to the north. "This place is too far gone. Is it any wonder we're leaving it behind?"

"You're the Voice of the Council," Palamon argued. "If you stay, the others will stay. Then together—"

"The decision has been made," Dossolum reminded him. "Some things cannot be redeemed. Some things shouldn't."

Palamon clenched his teeth against further argument. He still had entreaties to make. Better not to anger the only one who could grant his requests. But it was hard. He'd served those who lay dead in the streets below him, just as he'd served the Creation Council. *Someone* should speak for the dead.

"You don't have to stay," Dossolum offered again. "None of the Sheason need stay. There's little you can do here. What we began will run its course. You might slow it"—he looked back at the ruined city—"but eventually, it will all come to this."

Palamon shook his head again, this time in defiance. "You don't know that."

Dossolum showed him a patient look. "We don't go idly. The energy required to right this . . . Better to start fresh, with new matter. In another place." He looked up at evening stars showing in the east.

"Most of the Sheason are coming with you," Palamon admitted.

"All but you, I think." Dossolum dropped his gaze back to the city. "It's not going to be easy here. Even with the ability to render the Will . . ."

Palamon stared at burned stone and tracts of land blackened to nothing. "Because some of those who cross the Veil have the same authority," he observed.

"Not only that." Dossolum left it there.

"Then strengthen the Veil," Palamon pled. "Make it the protection you meant it to be." He put a hand on Dossolum's arm. "Please."

In the silence that followed, a soft sound touched the air. A song. A lament. Palamon shared a look with Dossolum, then followed the sound. They descended the low hill. And step by step the song grew louder, until they rounded a field home. Beside a shed near a blackened pasture sat a woman with her husband's head in her lap. She stroked his hair as she sang. Not loud. Not frantic. But anguished, like a deep, slow saddening moved through her.

Tears had cleaned tracks down her field-dirty cheeks. Or maybe it was char. Like the smell of burning all around them.

But she was alive. Palamon had thought everyone here dead.

She looked up at them, unsurprised. Her vacant stare might not have seen them at all. She kept singing.

Palamon noticed toys now beside the home.

"The city wasn't enough," Palamon said, anger welling inside him. "They came into the fields to get them all."

The woman sang on. Her somber melody floated like cottonwood seed, brushing past them soft and earthward.

Dossolum stood and listened a long while. He made no move to comfort the woman, or to revive the man. His face showed quiet appreciation. Only when she'd begun to repeat her song did he finally speak. And then in a low tone, like a counterpoint.

"Very well, Palamon." Dossolum continued to watch the woman grieve. "Write it all down. Everything we tried to do. Our failure. The Bourne and those we sent there. The war to do so." He grew quiet. "A story of desolation."

Tentatively, Palamon asked, "And do what with it?"

The woman's song turned low and throaty and bare.

Dossolum gave a sad smile. "To some we'll give a gift of song. They'll sing the story you write. And so long as they do, the Veil will be added to. Strengthened."

He nodded, seeming satisfied. "But it will be a suffering to sing it. Leaving them *diminished*."

"Thank you, Dossolum." Palamon then silently thanked the woman who mourned in front of them. Her mortal sorrow had touched his friend's eternal heart.

"Don't thank me." Dossolum's eyes showed their first hint of regret. "Like every good intention, a song can fade."

Palamon looked up at the same evening stars Dossolum had watched a moment ago. "Or it might be sung even after the light of the stars has fled the heavens."

"I hope you're right, my friend. I hope you're right."

BOOK ONE

THE UNREMEMBERED

STILLBORN

"The Church of Reconciliation—Reconciliationists, so called—preach that the Framers left behind protections. And these protections were given proper names. Names we've forgotten. Would these protections cease, then, to serve? Or would we have to question the origins of the doctrine?"

—Excerpt from *Rational Suppositions*,
a street tract disseminated by the League of Civility

A N OPEN DOOR ...

Tahn Junell drew his bow, and kicked his mount into a dead run. They descended the shallow dale in a rush toward that open door. Toward home.

The road was muddy. Hooves threw sludge. Lightning arced in the sky. A peal of thunder shattered the silence and pushed through the small vale in waves. It echoed outward through the woods in diminishing tolls.

The whispering sound of rain on trees floated toward him. The soft smells of earth and pollen hung on the air, charged with the coming of another storm. Cold perspiration beaded on his forehead and neck.

An open door . . .

His sister, Wendra, wouldn't leave the door open to the chill.

Passing the stable, another bolt of white fire erupted from the sky, this time striking the ground. It hit at the near end of the vale. Thunder exploded around him. A moment later, a scream rose from inside his home. His mount reared, tugging at his reins and throwing Tahn to the ground before racing for the safety of the stable. Tahn lost his bow and began frantically searching the mud for the dropped weapon. The sizzle of falling rain rose, a lulling counterpoint to the screams that continued from inside. Something crashed to the floor of the cabin. Then a wail rose up. It sounded at once deep in the throat, like the thunder, and high in the nose like a child's mirth.

Tahn's heart drummed in his ears and neck and chest. His throat throbbed with it. Wendra was in there! He found his bow. Shaking the mud and water from the bowstring and quickly cleaning the arrow's fletching on his coat, he sprinted for the door. He nocked the arrow and leapt to the stoop.

The home had grown suddenly still and quiet.

He burst in, holding his aim high and loose.

An undisturbed fire burned in the hearth, but everything else in his home lay strewn or broken. The table had been toppled on its side, earthen plates broken into shards across the floor. Food was splattered against one wall and puddled near a cooking pot in the far corner. Wendra's few books sat partially burned near the fire, their thrower's aim not quite sure. Tahn saw it all in a glance as he swung his bow to the left where Wendra had tucked her bed up under the loft.

She lay atop her quilts, knees up and legs spread.

Absent gods, no!

Then, within the shadows beneath the loft, Tahn saw it, a hulking mass standing at the foot of Wendra's bed. It hunched over, too tall to remain upright in the nook beneath the upper room. Its hands cradled something in a blanket of horsehair. The smell of sweat and blood and new birth commingled with the aroma of the cooking pot.

The figure slowly turned its massive head toward him. Wendra looked too, her eyes weary but alive with fright. She weakly reached one arm toward him, mouthing something, but unable to speak.

In a low, guttural voice the creature spoke, "*Quillescent all around.*" It rasped words in thick, glottal tones.

Then it stepped from beneath the loft, its girth massive. The fire lit the creature's fibrous skin, which moved independent of the muscle and bone beneath. Ridges and rills marked its hide, which looked like elm bark. But pliable. It uncoiled its left arm from the blanket it held to its chest, letting its hand hang nearly to its knees. From a leather sheath strapped to its leg, the figure drew a long knife. Around the hilt it curled its hand—three talonlike fingers with a thumb on each side, its palm as large as Tahn's face. Then it pointed the blade at him.

Tahn's legs began to quiver. Revulsion and fear pounded in his chest. This was a nightmare come to life. This was Bar'dyn, a race out of the Bourne. One of those given to Quietus, the dissenting god.

"We go," the Quietgiven said evenly. It spoke deep in its throat. Its speech belied a sharp intelligence in its eyes. When it spoke, only its lips moved. The skin on its face remained thick and still, draped loosely over protruding cheekbones that jutted like shelves beneath its eyes. Tahn glimpsed a mouthful of sharp teeth.

"Tahn," Wendra managed, her voice hoarse and afraid.

Blood spots marked her white bed-dress, and her body seemed frozen in a position that prevented her from straightening her legs. Tahn's heart stopped.

Against its barklike skin, the Bar'dyn held cradled in a tightly woven blanket of mane and tail . . . Wendra's child.

Pressure mounted in Tahn's belly: hate, helplessness, confusion, fear. All a madness like panicked wings in his mind. He was supposed to protect her, keep her safe, especially while she carried this child. A child come of rape. But a child she looked forward to. Loved.

Worry and anger rushed inside him. "No!"

His scream filled the small cabin, leaving a deeper silence in its wake. But the babe made no sound. The Bar'dyn only stared. On the stoop and roof, the patter of rain resumed, like the sound of a distant waterfall. Beyond it, Tahn heard the gallop of hooves on the muddy road. *More Bar'dyn? His friends?*

He couldn't wait for either. In a shaky motion, he drew his aim on the creature's head. The Bar'dyn didn't move. There wasn't even defiance in its expression.

"I'll take you *and* the child. Velle will be pleased." It nodded at its own words, then raised its blade between them.

Velle? Dead gods, they've brought a renderer of the Will with them!

Tahn's aim floundered from side to side. Weariness. Cold fear.

The Bar'dyn stepped toward him. Tahn's mind raced, and fastened upon one thought. *The hammer.* He focused on that mark on the back of his bow hand, visually tracing its lines and feeling it with his mind. A simple, solid thing. He didn't remember where he'd gotten the scar or brand, but it seemed intentional. And it grounded him. With that moment of reassurance, his hands steadied, and he drew deeper into the pull, bringing his aim on the Bar'dyn's throat.

"Put the child down." His voice trembled even as his mouth grew dry.

The Bar'dyn paused, looking down at the bundle it carried. The creature then lifted the babe up, causing the blanket to slip to the floor. Its massive hand curled around the little one's torso. The infant still glistened from its passage out of Wendra's body, its skin red and purple in the sallow light of the fire.

"Child came dead, grub."

Sadness and anger welled again in Tahn. His chest heaved at the thought of Wendra giving birth in the company of this vile thing, having her baby taken at the moment of life into its hands. *Was the child dead at birth, or had the Bar'dyn killed it?* Tahn glanced again at Wendra. She was pale. Sadness etched her features. He watched her close her eyes against the Bar'dyn's words.

The rain now pounded the roof. But the sound of heavy footfalls on the road was clear, close, and Tahn abandoned hope of escape. One Bar'dyn, let alone several, might tear him apart, but he intended to send this one to the abyss, for Wendra, for her dead child.

He prepared to fire his bow, allowing time enough to speak the old, familiar words: "I draw with the strength of my arms, but release as the Will allows."

But he couldn't shoot.

He struggled to disobey the feeling, but it stretched back into that part of his life he couldn't remember. He had always spoken the words, always. He didn't release of his own choice. He always followed the quiet intimations that came after he spoke those words.

Tahn relaxed his aim and the Bar'dyn nodded approval. "Bound to Will," it said. The words rang like the cracking of timber in the confines of the small home. "But first to watch this one go." The Bar'dyn turned toward Wendra.

"No!" Tahn screamed again, filling the cabin with denial. Denial of the Bar'dyn.

Denial of his own impotence.

The sound of others came up the steps. Tahn was surrounded. They would all die!

He spared a last look at his sister. "I'm sorry," he tried to say, but it came out in a husk.

Her expression of confusion and hurt and disappointment sank deep inside him.

If he couldn't kill the creature, he could at least try to prevent it from hurting her.

Before he could move, his friends shot through the door. They got between Tahn and the Bar'dyn. They fought the creature. They filled his home with a clash of wills and swordplay and shouted oaths. Chaos churned around him. And all he could do was watch Wendra curl deeper into her bed. Afraid. Heartsick.

The creature out of the Bourne finally turned and crashed through the cabin's rear wall, rushing into the dark and the storm with Wendra's dead child. They did not give chase.

Tahn turned from the hole in the wall and went to Wendra's side. Blood soaked the coverlet, and cuts in her wrists and hands told of failed attempts to ward off the Bar'dyn. Her cheeks sagged; she looked pale and spent. She lay crying silent tears.

He'd stood twenty feet away with a clear shot at the Bar'dyn and had done nothing. The lives of his sister and her child had hung in the balance, and he'd done nothing. The old words had told him the draw was wrong. He'd followed that feeling over the defense of his sister. Why?

It was an old ache and frustration, believing himself bound to the impressions those words stirred inside him. But never so much as now.

CHAPTER ONE

OLD WORDS

"It is the natural condition of man to strive for certainty. It is also his condition not to find it. Not for long, anyway. Even a star may wander."

> —From *Commentary on Categoricals,*
> a reader for children nominated to
> Dimnian cognitive training

TRANQUIL DARKNESS STRETCHED to the horizon. Small hours. Moments of quiet, of peace. Moments when faraway stars seemed as close and familiar as friends. Moments of night before the east would hint of sunrise. Tahn stepped into these small hours. Into the chill night air. He went to spend time with the stars. To imagine dawn. As he always had.

There was a kind of song in it all. A predictable rhythm and melody that might only be heard by one willing to remain quiet and unmoving long enough to note the movement of a star. It could be heard in the phases of the moons. It was by turns a single deep sonorous note, large as a russet sun setting slow, and then a great chorus, as when showers of shooting stars brightened the night sky. They were harmonies across ages, heard during the brief measure of a life. But only if one paused, as Tahn did, to watch and listen.

He stood at the edge of the High Plains of Sedagin. The bluff rose a thousand strides off the flatlands below. Stars winked like sparkling bits of glass on a dark tablecloth. His breath clouded the night, and droplets hung like frozen tears from low scrub and sage.

He looked east and let his thoughts come naturally. Deep into the far reaches of the sky he let them wander, his emotions and hopes struggling for form with the stars. He traced the constellations, some from old stories, some from memories whose sources were lost to him. A half-full moon had risen high, its surface bright and clear. The pale outline of the darkened portion appeared a ghostly halo.

Tahn closed his eyes and let his thoughts run out even further, imagining the sun; imagining its warmth and radiance, its calm, sure track across the heavens. He imagined the sky changing color in the east from black to violet to sea blue and finally the color of clear, shallow water. He pictured more color as sunlight came to the forest and touched its leaves and cones and limbs. He envisioned those first moments of dawn, the unfurling of flower petals to its light, its glint on rippling water, steam rising from warming loam. And as he always did at such a moment, Tahn felt like part of the land, another leaf to be touched by the sun. His thoughts coalesced into the singular moment of sunrise and another hope risen up from the night, born again with quiet strength.

He opened his eyes to the dark skies and the foliate pattern of stars. In the east, the first intimation of day arose as the black hinted of violet hues. A quiet relief filled him, and he took a lungful of air.

Another day would come. And pass. Until the beautiful, distant stars returned, and he came again to watch. Until someday, when either he or the sun would not rise. And the song would end.

He lingered, enjoying a moment's peace. They'd been on the road more days than he could remember. Chased by the Quiet. Chased since the night he'd let Wendra down, failed to shoot when she'd needed him, when the Quiet took her child. Tahn shook his head with guilt at the memory of it.

And now here he was. Weeks later. Far from home. Just tonight they'd climbed this plateau, arriving after midnight. After dark hour.

He took a long breath, relaxing in the stillness.

The sound of boots over frost-covered earth startled him. He turned to see Vendanj come to join him.

Even the shadows of night couldn't soften the hard edges of the man. Vendanj wore determination the way another does his boots. Carried it in his eyes and shoulders. Vendanj was a member of the Sheason Order, those who rendered the Will—that melding of spirit and body, energy and matter. The

Sheason weren't well known in the Hollows, Tahn's home. And Tahn was learning that beyond the Hollows, the Sheason weren't always welcome. Were even distrusted.

Vendanj came up beside him, and stared out over the plains far and away below. He didn't rush to clutter the silence with words. And they watched together for a time.

After long moments, Vendanj eyed Tahn with wry suspicion. "You do this every morning." It wasn't a question.

Tahn returned the wry grin. "How would you know? You follow me everywhere?"

"Just until we reach the Saeculorum," Vendanj answered.

They shared quiet laughter over that. It was a rare jest from Vendanj. But it was a square jest, the kind with truth inside. Because they were, in fact, going to the Saeculorum—mountains at the far end of the Eastlands. Several months' travel from here.

"For as long as I can remember," Tahn finally admitted, "I've gotten up early to watch the sunrise. Habit now, I guess."

Vendanj folded his arms as he stared east. "It's more than a habit, I suspect."

And he was right. It was more like a compulsion. A need. To stand with the stars. Imagine daybreak.

But Vendanj didn't press, and fell silent again for a time.

Into the silence, distantly, came again the sound of footfalls over hard dirt. The chill air grew . . . tight. Dense. It seemed to press on Tahn. Panic tightened his gut. Vendanj held up a hand for Tahn not to speak. A few moments later, up the trail of the cliff face came a figure, unhurried. Directly toward them.

Soon, the moon brought the shape into focus. A man. He wore an unremarkable coat, buttoned high against the chill. No cowl or robe or weapon. No smile of greeting. No frown. It was the man's utter lack of expression that frightened Tahn most, as if feeling had gone out of him.

Twenty strides from them, the other stopped, returning the bluff to silence. The figure stared at them through the dark. Stared at them with disregard.

Softer than a whisper, "Velle," Vendanj said.

My dying gods.

Velle were Quiet renderers of the Will. Like Sheason, but followers of the dissenting god.

The silence stretched between them, dawn still a long while away.

Into the stillness, the other spoke, his voice soft and low. "Your legs will tire, Sheason. And we will be there when they do." He pointed at Tahn. "Send me the boy, and let's be done."

"It would do you no good," Vendanj replied. "If not the boy, there are others."

The Velle nodded. "We know. And this one isn't the first you've driven like a mule." The man's eyes shifted to Tahn. "What has he told you, Quillescent?"

Tahn didn't really understand the question, and didn't reply. He only took his bow down from his shoulder.

The Velle shook his head slowly in disappointment. "You don't have the energy to fight me, Sheason. You've spent too much already."

"I appreciate your concern," Vendanj said, another surprising jest from the usually severe man.

The Velle hadn't taken its eyes from Tahn. "And what about you, with your little bow? Are you going to ask your gods if I should die, and shoot me down?" The expression in the man's face changed, but only by degrees. *More* indifferent. Careworn to the bone, beyond feeling.

He knows. He knows the words I speak when I draw.

The Velle dropped its chin. "Ask it." The words were an invitation, a challenge. And the chill air bristled when the Velle spoke them. Grasses and low sage bent away from the man as though they would flee.

Vendanj held up a hand. "You've strolled onto the Sedagin plain, my Quiet friend. A thousand swords and more. Go back the way you came."

A slow smile touched the Velle's face. A wan smile lacking warmth or humor. And even that looked unnatural, as though he were unaccustomed to smiling at all. "I don't take care for myself, Sheason. That is a *man's* weakness. And there'll be no heroes this time." He raised a hand, and Vendanj let out an explosive exhale, as if his chest were suddenly being pressed by boulders.

In a single motion, Tahn raised his bow and drew an arrow. *I draw with the strength of my arms, but release as the Will allows.*

The quiet confirmation came. The Velle should die.

Tahn caught a glimpse of a more genuine smile on the Quiet's lips before he let his arrow fly. An unconcerned flip of the Velle's wrist, and the arrow careened high and harmless out over the bluff's edge.

Vendanj dropped to his knees, struggling against some unseen force. Tahn had to disrupt the Velle's hold on the Sheason somehow. But before he could move, a deep shiver started in his chest as though his body were a low cello string being slowly played. And with the resonance rushed the memory of his failure to shoot the Bar'dyn that had come into his and Wendra's home, taken her child.

Except it seemed more raw now. Like alcohol poured on a fresh cut.

And that wasn't all. Other memories stirred. Lies he'd told. Insults he'd offered. Though he couldn't recall them with exactness. They were half formed, but sharpening.

He was maybe seven. A fight. Friends. Some kind of contest to settle . . .

Tahn began to tremble violently. His teeth ached and felt ready to shatter. His mind burned hot with regret and self-loathing. He dropped face-first beside Vendanj, and curled into a ball against the pain.

Vendanj still wasn't breathing, but managed to thrust an open palm at the Velle. The Quiet man grimaced, and Vendanj drew a harsh-sounding breath, his face slick with sweat in the moonlight.

Tahn's own inner ache subsided, and the quaking in his body stopped. Briefly. The Velle dropped to both knees and drove its hands into the hard soil. Blackness flared, and the Quiet man looked suddenly refreshed. This time, it simply stared at Vendanj. The earth between them whipped, low sage tearing away. But Vendanj was prepared, and kept his feet and breath when some force hit him, exploding in a fury of spent energy. The Sheason's lean face had drawn into a grim expression, and he began shaking his head.

The Velle glanced at Tahn and tremors wracked his body again. With them came his insecurities about childhood years lost to memory. As if they didn't matter. As if *he* didn't matter, except to raise his bow and repeat those godsforsaken words, *I draw with the strength* . . .

As the Velle caressed him with this deep resonant pain, a shadow flashed behind the other. Light and quick.

A moment later the Velle's back arched, his eyes wide in surprise. Tahn's tremors stopped. Vendanj lowered his arms. The Velle fell forward, and standing there was Mira Far, of the Far people. Her pale skin awash in moonlight. Only a Far could have gotten behind a Velle without being noticed. Looking at her, Tahn felt a different kind of tug inside. One that was altogether more appealing.

For the third time that morning, boots over hard earth interrupted the dark morning stillness. A hundred strides behind Mira three Bar'dyn emerged on the trail. At first they only walked. Then, seeing the downed Velle, they broke into a run, a kind of reasoned indifference in their faces. Their massive frames moved with grace, and power, as their feet pounded against the cold earth.

Tahn reached for an arrow. Mira dropped into one of her Latae stances, both swords raised. Vendanj gasped several breaths, still trying to steady himself from his contest with the Velle. "Take the Bar'dyn down," he said, his voice full of hateful prejudice.

Tahn pulled three successive draws, thinking the old words in an instant and firing at the closest Bar'dyn. The first arrow bounded harmlessly off the creature's barklike skin. But the next two struck it in the neck. It fell with a heavy crunch on the frost-covered soil.

The remaining two descended on Mira first. She ducked under a savage swipe of a long rounded blade and came up with a thrust into the creature's groin. Not simply an attack on its tender parts, but a precise cut into the artery that ran alongside them—something she'd taught him during one of their many conversations.

The Bar'dyn shrugged off the blow and rushed onward toward Tahn. In a few moments it would grow sluggish from blood loss, and finally fall. Tahn had only to keep a distance.

The other Quiet pushed ahead faster, closing on Tahn. Mira took chase, but even with her gift of speed wouldn't reach it before it got to him. Tahn pulled a deep draw. The Bar'dyn raised a forearm to protect its neck, and barreled closer.

"Take it down!" Vendanj began raising a hand, clearly weakened. The Sheason had rendered the Will so often lately. And he'd had little time to recover.

Tahn breathed out, steadied his aim, spoke the words in his mind, and let fly. The arrow hit true, taking the Bar'dyn's left eye. No cry or scream. It stutter-stepped, and kept on. Its expression was as impassive as before—not fury, reason.

Tahn drew again. This arrow struck the Quiet's knee, as he'd intended. But it shattered against the armor-hard skin there. It was almost too close to fire again, but Tahn pulled a quick draw, Mira a half step behind the creature, and fired at its mouth. The arrow smashed through its teeth and went out through its cheek. The Bar'dyn's face stretched in a mask of pain. Then it leveled its eyes again and leapt at Tahn.

It was too late to avoid the Quiet. Tahn braced himself. The massive creature drove him to the ground under its immense weight. Tahn lost his breath, couldn't cry out. He could feel blood on his face. The Bar'dyn shifted to take hold of him.

It propped itself up with one arm, and stared down at Tahn with its indifferent eyes. "You don't understand," it said with a thick, glottal voice.

The Bar'dyn began to roll, pulling Tahn with it, as if it might try to carry him away. A moment later, it stopped moving. Mira. She pulled her blade from the creature's head. Then she turned on the wounded Bar'dyn, who was now staggering toward them, weak from loss of blood.

The last Quiet fell. It panted for several moments, then went still.

CHAPTER TWO

KEEPING PROMISES

"And a Sheason known as Portis came into the court of King Yusefi, king of Kuren, and demanded he keep his pledge to the Second Promise and send men to help the Sedagin in the far North. But Yusefi denied him. Whereupon Portis rendered the king's blood boiling hot and burned him alive inside. To my knowledge, this is the first recorded instance of Sheason violence against man."

—An account of the Castigation, from the pages of the Kuren Court diarist

WARM BAR'DYN BLOOD steamed in the moonlight. Tahn scrambled away from the dead Quiet and sat heavily on the cold ground. His heart hammered in his chest. There was no getting used to this.

And now a Velle! What had it done to him? He still felt it. Like vibrations of thought or emotion. Deep down.

"All the way to the Saeculorum," Tahn said, repeating the joke Vendanj had made before this latest Quiet attack. Now it just sounded exhausting. Impossible.

Vendanj eased himself down to sit near Tahn. "It's good you're handy with a bow."

Mira crouched in front of them, keeping her feet under her—always ready. "Velle. That's new." She was looking at Vendanj.

He nodded. "But not surprising. And not the last we'll see of them."

"There's a happy thought," Tahn said without humor. "Seems like every damn day another storybook rhyme steps from the page. What was it doing to me?"

Vendanj eyed him. Tapped his own chest. "You felt it in here."

Tahn nodded.

"A renderer of the Will can move things," he explained. "Push them. Sometimes you'll see what he does. Sometimes you won't." He took a long breath. "Sometimes it's outside the body. And other times," Vendanj tapped his chest again, "it's in here."

"I don't feel the same," Tahn said.

"It's Resonance." Vendanj said it with obvious concern. "It'll linger like a played note. Won't ever go away completely. But it'll stop feeling like it does today."

Tahn rubbed his chest. "I felt like I was remembering. . . ." But it hadn't completely come back. Mostly the *feeling* of the memory remained. He turned to Vendanj. "What did it mean, 'There'll be no heroes this time'?"

Vendanj took a storyteller's breath. "This plateau used to be part of the flatlands below." He gestured out over the bluff. "The Sedagin people here are known as the Right Arm of the Promise. Masters of the longblade. They've always kept the First Promise; always marched against the Quiet when they come."

"What about this time?" Tahn asked, looking at the dead Velle.

Vendanj didn't seem to hear him. "First time the Quiet came, the regent of Recityv called a Convocation of Seats. Every nation and throne was asked to join an alliance to meet the threat. And most did. The Sedagin were the strongest part of that army. And the Quiet were pushed back.

"Ages later, the Quiet came again." Vendanj shook his head and sighed. "But by then Convocation had become a political game. Kings committed only token regiments. So, the regent Corihehn adjourned Convocation and sent word to Holivagh, leader of the Sedagin, to march toward the Pall mountains. He told him there was a Second Promise from this Second Convocation. He told him an alliance army would meet them there."

Tahn guessed the next part, disgust rising in his throat. "It was a lie."

"It was a lie," Vendanj echoed, nodding. "Twenty thousand Sedagin soldiers cut a path through the Quiet. They reached the Pall mountains where Bourne armies were crossing into the Eastlands, but by then only two thousand Sedagin were left. Still, they held the breach for eight days. They waited for Corihehn's reinforcements. But the army of the

Second Promise never came. And every Sedagin bladesman perished."

"But we won the war," Tahn added, tentative.

"When Del'Agio, Randeur of the Sheason, learned what Corihehn had done, he sent Sheason messengers into the courts of every city. They threatened death to any who wouldn't honor Corihehn's lie. The Castigation, it was called."

Vendanj looked up and down the edge of the bluff. "When the war was won, the Sheason came into the high plains. For several cycles of the first moon they linked hands and willed the earth to rise, built an earthen monument to the Sedagin. Gave them a home. These plains are known as Teheale. It means 'earned in blood' in the Covenant Tongue."

Tahn sat silent in reverence to the sacrifice made so long ago.

"Seems our Velle friend doesn't think Sheason and Sedagin can turn the Quiet back again." Vendanj's smile caught in the light of the moon. "No heroes."

In many ways, Vendanj reminded Tahn of his father, Balatin. Serious, but able to let worry go when he sensed Tahn needed to laugh or just let things lie. Tahn suddenly missed his father, a deep missing. His da had gone to his earth a few years ago, leaving Tahn and Wendra to make their way alone—their mother, Vocencia, had died a few years before Balatin. He missed her, too.

"It'll look something like this." Vendanj gestured away from the high plateau again, shifting topics. "The Heights of Restoration, Tahn. On the far side of the Saeculorum."

"Because you think this time *I'm* the hero?" He stared at the steam rising from the dead Bar'dyn's wounds.

Vendanj sighed. "I'm inclined to agree with the Velle. And I don't think like that anymore." He paused, his eyes distant. "If I ever did."

"He said there were others," Tahn pressed. "Called me a mule."

Vendanj gave a dismissive laugh over that. "We're all mules. Each hauling some damn load, don't you think?"

Tahn waited, making clear he wanted an answer. He'd agreed to come. He was bone weary, and scared to think Vendanj had pinned too much hope on him.

Tahn could hit almost anything with his bow. There'd been countless hours of practice supervised by his father. Even before that, he'd had a sure hand.

Somewhere in those lost years of his young life he'd obviously learned its use; fighting techniques, too—his reactions were like Mira's Latae battle forms, just less polished. But against an army? Against Velle? That thing had taken hold of him somehow. Not just his body, but *who* he was. It had stroked painful memories, giving them new life in his mind. It was a pain unlike anything he'd yet felt. This was madness.

What the hell am I doing?

The Sheason seemed to know his thoughts, and put a hand on Tahn's shoulder. "There's a sense about you, Tahn. Like the words you use when you draw your bow." He paused. "But no, you're not the only one we've taken to Restoration.

Remember what I said at the start: We believe you can stand there. You've not passed your Change, so the burdens of your mistakes aren't fully on you yet. That'll make it easier."

"Why would you need *me* if you've taken others?"

Vendanj let out a long breath. He settled a gaze on Tahn that spoke of disappointment and regret. "None have survived Tillinghast." He paused as if weighing Tahn's resolve. "That's its old name. Tillinghast is where the Heights of Restoration fall away." He gestured again toward the cliff's edge close by. "Like this bluff."

Before Tahn could comment, Vendanj pushed on. "And that's those who went at all. Most chose not to go. Your willingness. It sets you apart from most."

"He's right," Mira added, approval in her voice.

Tahn looked up at her, finding encouragement in her silver-grey eyes. She showed him the barest of smiles. And warmth flooded his chest and belly, chasing out some of the deep shiver still lingering inside him.

"Tahn," Vendanj said, gathering his attention again. "The thing you need to remember is this. Standing at Tillinghast isn't just about what ever mettle's in you to survive its touch. It's more about whether or not you can suffer the change it'll cause in you once it's done."

Tahn shook his head, panic fluttering anew in his chest. "What change?"

"Different for everyone who stands there," Vendanj replied.

"If they *live*," Tahn observed with sharp sarcasm. "And then do what?"

"If the Quiet fully break free of the Bourne"—Mira nodded as though it was only a matter of time—"they'll come with elder beings. Creatures against which steel is useless."

Vendanj got to his feet. "And my order is at odds with itself. Diminished because of it." He looked down at Tahn. "This time . . . we've asked *you* to go to Tillinghast. The Veil that holds the Quiet at bay is weakening. Could be that the Song of Suffering that keeps it strong is failing. I know there are few with the ability to sing Suffering. But whatever the reason for the Veil's weakness, we think—if you can stand at Tillinghast—you can help should a full Quiet army come."

Tahn shook his head in disbelief. And fear. "All because of the damned words I can't help but say every time I draw." He shook his bow. "And because I have a *sense*. Maybe it's time you restore my memory. Give me back those twelve years you say you took from me when you sent me to the Hollows."

He wanted that more than he let on. His earliest memories began just six years ago. *Twelve years. Gone.* And until Vendanj had come into the Hollows, Than had thought maybe he'd had some sort of accident. Hit his head. Lost his memory. But the Sheason had taken it. To protect him, the man had said.

"You may believe you're ready for that. But think about it." He pointed at the Velle, which had surfaced searing memories in him. "You don't remember your young life

. . . but it was a hard one. Not *all* hard. But most of it was spent in an unhappy place. And now, you're far from home, chased by Quiet, asked to climb to Tillinghast, and you're coming soon to the age of accountability."

Tahn had been eager for his Standing and the Change that came after his eighteenth year. Eager for what, he didn't exactly know. To be taken more seriously was part of it, though. And because he'd thought he might somehow get his memory back.

Tahn stood, shouldered his bow. "Wouldn't that suggest I'm old enough—"

"No, it wouldn't," Vendanj cut in sharply. "I took your memory all those years ago as a protection to you. It still is. Before we reach Tillinghast I'll return it to you. You'll need it there." He put his hand again on Tahn's shoulder, his hard expression softening. "But not now. Trust me on this. I've seen what it does to a mind when so much change comes at once."

Tahn thought about the pressure in his body and mind when the Velle had taken hold of him. The things it had surfaced all in a rush. Jagged, ugly things to remember.

Images of young friends, though he couldn't see their faces. A fight, though he couldn't remember why. Except they were settling something. The feeling of betrayal lingered. A sad pain in the pit of his stomach.

Tahn walked to where the Velle lay. Something glinted on the ground near its body. He hunkered down and ran his fingers across a smooth surface glistening with moonlight. Felt like glass. At its center were two fist-sized holes.

"What's this?"

Vendanj came up beside him. "Velle won't bear the cost of rendering the Will. They transfer it. Take the vitality of anything at hand so they can remain strong."

The Velle had thrust its hands into the soil. Darkness had flared. It had caused the formation of this thin crust of dark glass. Tahn stepped on it. A soft *pop*. A fragile sound. If Vendanj hadn't been here, what else inside Tahn would the Velle have taken hold of?

He finally gave a low, resigned laugh. "You win. Why complicate all this fun we're having, right?"

He stole a look at Mira, who showed him her slim smile again. That, at least, was helpful. Hopeful, too. Like the lighter shades of blue strengthening in the east behind her.

Just before he turned away, he caught sight of low fogs gathering on the lowland floor. He pointed. "You see that?"

Vendanj looked, and his expression hardened. Soon Mira stood with them, as they watched a cloud bank form around the base of the plateau.

"Je'holta," Vendanj said.

"What is it?" Tahn asked.

"Another form of Quiet." He paused a long moment. "And something we'll now have to pass through when we leave here."

Mira's smile was gone. "Good test for Tillinghast."

Tahn gave them each a long look, and said without humor, "I just came out to watch the sunrise. . . ."

Read on for a preview of the

TRIAL OF INTENTIONS

BOOK TWO OF
THE VAULT OF HEAVEN

by

PETER ORULLIAN

TRIAL OF INTENTIONS

P R O L O G U E

A THIRD PURPOSE

"Encouragements are drawn from living things—trees, grasses, animals. First and best from family. All are vital. All nourish. Perishment results from the absence of these."
—From *The Effect of Absences*, a correlative war doctrine originating in the Bourne

AFTER LONG YEARS in the Scarred Lands, Tahn Junell realized their patrols held a third purpose.

First, and most obviously, they were meant to provide early warning when visitors or strangers came into the Scar. Patrol routes held long sight lines of the wide, barren lands. From a distance, newcomers could be easily spotted and reported.

On a second, more practical level, patrols were used to build and maintain stamina for fight sessions. Every ward of the Scar—age three to nineteen—spent no less than six hours a day in ritualized combat training.

It wasn't until later that Tahn finally came to realize a subtle third reason for patrols. They were a way for wards of the

Scar to monitor themselves and guard against one of their own wandering from home, alone.

With the purpose of self-slaughter.

Tahn and Alemdra ran fast, arriving at Gutter Ridge well ahead of sunrise. They slowed to a walk, catching their breath and sharing smiles.

"You're starting to slow me down," Alemdra teased. "I think it's because I'm becoming a woman, and you're still a boy."

He laughed. "Well, maybe if we're going to keep running patrols together, I'll just put a saddle on you, then."

She hit him in the arm, and they sat together with their legs dangling from one of the few significant ridges in the Scar. Alemdra was twelve today, barely older than Tahn. And he intended to kiss her. Seeing the glint in her eye, he wondered if she'd guessed his intention. But if so, the unspoken secret only added to the anticipation.

Casually wagging their toes, they looked east.

"See that?" He pointed at the brightest star in the eastern hemisphere. She nodded. "That's Katia Shonay, the morning star. It's really a planet."

"That so." She squinted as if doing so might bring the distant object into sharper focus.

"Katia Shonay means 'lovelorn' in Dimnian." He liked few things better than talking about the sky. "There's this whole story about how a furrow tender fell in love with a woman of the court."

She made no effort to conceal her suspicion of his timing for sharing the story of this particular planet. "You might make a good furrow tender someday. If you work hard at it, that is."

"Actually," he countered, smiling, "the story's only complete in the conjunction of Rushe Symone—the planet named after the god of plenty and favor. You know, bountiful harvests and autumn bacchanalia." He nearly blushed over the last part, having learned the richness of bacchanal rituals. "Rych is the largest planet—"

She was giving him a look. *The* look. "You seem to think you're smarter than us now."

"What do you mean *now*?" And he started laughing.

She broke down laughing, too. "You really liked it there, didn't you? In Aubade Grove."

"I'd go back tomorrow if it didn't mean leaving you behind." It came out sounding more honest than he'd intended, but he wasn't embarrassed. He stared off at Katia. "It's amazing, Alemdra. No patrols. No fight sessions. Just books. Study. Skyglassing to discover what's up there." He gestured grandly at the eastern sky.

She smiled, sharing his enthusiasm for the few years he'd been away before being called back here. "Do you think you'll ever leave the Scar for good?" There was a small, fatal note in her voice.

He turned to see her expression—the same one she always wore when they talked about Grant. While all the wards were like Grant's adoptive children, Tahn was the man's actual son. He supposed someday he might leave this place, especially if he ever learned who his mother was. If she was still alive.

"Eventually. After my father goes to his earth. I don't think I could leave him here alone." Tahn threw a rock and listened for it to hit far below. In his head he began doing some math to determine the height of the ridge. *Initial velocity, count of six to the rock's impact, acceleration due to gravity—*

"He'll never be alone, Tahn," she said, interrupting his calculations. "Not as long as the *cradle* is here."

Tahn nodded grimly. The Forgotten Cradle. It served as a big damn reminder of abandonment to all the wards of the Scar. And it was how most of them came to this place. Every cycle of the first moon a babe was placed in the hollow of a dead bristlecone pine. Orphans. Foundlings. And sometimes children whose parents just didn't want them anymore. Grant retrieved each child, tried to find it a proper home outside the Scar. Those for whom no arrangements could be made came to live with them *inside* the Scar. Not knowing their actual day of birth, wards celebrated their "cradleday"—the day they were rescued from the tree. Like he and Alemdra were doing for her today.

"I don't know why you feel any loyalty to stay, either." She looked away to where the sun would crest the mountains to the east. "Not after what he's done to you."

His father put more pressure on him. Tahn's lessons were less predictable. Harder. One might wonder if being his son, he bore the brunt of his father's exile here. A sentence he'd earned for defying the regent. And his father could never leave; otherwise who would fetch the babes from the cradle?

Their special morning had struck a somber note. But he couldn't let her comment lie, even though in his heart he agreed. "He just has a different way of teaching."

Alemdra seemed to realize she'd touched too close to private insecurities. "If you go, will you take me with you?"

Tahn smiled, grateful for a change in the direction of their morning chat. "You think you can keep up? I mean, I *have* been off to college and all."

This time she hit him in the shoulder, soft enough to let him know she wasn't offended, hard enough to let him know she was no rube. Then they fell into another companionable silence. The sun was near to rising. They wouldn't speak again until its rays glimmered in their eyes. This was Tahn's favorite time in the Scar. Morning had a kind of wonder in it. As if the day might end differently than the one before it. That moment of sun first lighting the sky was something he made time every day to witness. And he liked these sunrise moments best when Alemdra was with him.

He wanted to kiss her when the sun began to break. Sentimental, maybe, but it felt right anyway. As the time drew closer, his left leg began to shimmy all on its own.

What if he'd misread their growing friendship? What if she rejected his kiss? He'd be ruining future chances to run with her on morning patrol.

When the sun's first rays broke over the horizon, he turned to her, his mind racing to find some words, debating if he should just grasp her by the shoulders and do it.

He neither spoke nor grasped. In the second he turned, Alemdra inclined with a swift grace and put her mouth on his. Her eyes were open, and she left her lips there for a long time before closing them and uttering a sigh of innocent delight.

The sound brought Tahn's heart to a pounding thump, and he knew he loved her. The other wards would tease him; maybe try to convince him he was just a boy and couldn't know such feelings. Let them. Because even if he and Alemdra never knew a more intimate moment than this, he would always remember her kiss, her sigh.

Sometime later, she pulled away, her eyes opening again. She smiled—not with embarrassment, but happily. And together they watched the sun finish its rise into the sky.

Then an urgent rhythm interrupted the morning stillness. Distant footfalls. Someone running. Together they turned toward the sound. A hundred strides to the east, from behind a copse of dead trees, a figure emerged at a dead run toward the cliff. They watched in horror as their friend Devin leapt from the edge. Her arms and legs pinwheeled briefly, before she gave in to the fall, her body pulled earthward toward the jag of rocks far below.

Alemdra screamed. The shrill sound echoed across the deep, rocky ravine as their friend fell down. And down. Tahn stood up on impulse, but could only watch as Devin stared skyward, letting the force of attraction do its awful work. *Initial velocity, acceleration due to gravity . . .*

A few moments later, Devin struck the hardpan below with a sharp cry. And lay instantly still.

"Devin!" Tahn wailed, wanting his friend to take it back. Angry, frustrated tears filled his eyes.

Alemdra turned to him. They shared a long, painful look. They'd failed their third purpose. They'd been so caught up in Alemdra's cradleday, in the peace of sunrise, in their first kiss, that they'd missed any signs of Devin. One of their closest friends.

Alemdra sank to her knees, sobs wracking her body. Tahn put his arms around her and together they wept for Devin. At Gutter Ridge, in the first rays of day, with Katia Shonay still rising in the east, they wept for another ward who'd lost her battle with the Scar.

The third purpose. Tahn understood the feeling that got into those who made this choice. Every ward had some kind of defense against it. Or tried. His defense was the sky, morning and sunrise. Those moments gave him something to look forward to, to find hope in.

Sometime later, they started down to gather the body, keeping a griever's silence as they went. The sun had grown hot by the time they got to Devin. They stood a while before Alemdra broke the silence. "She turned fifteen last week."

Wards who found their way out of the Scar often did so soon after their cradleday.

Alemdra sniffed, wiping away tears. There was a familiar worry in her voice when she whispered, "She was strong. Stronger than most."

Tahn knew she meant in spirit. He nodded. "That's what scares me."

They fell silent again, knowing soon enough they'd need to build a litter to drag the body home. There'd be a note in Devin's pocket. There was always a note. It would speak of apology. Of regret. Of the inability to suffer the Scar another day. There'd be no blame laid on Grant. Actually, he'd be thanked for caring for them, for trying to teach them to survive in the world. But mostly, the note would be about what *wasn't* written on the paper. It would be about how the Scar somehow amplified the abandonment that had brought a ward to the Forgotten Cradle in the first place.

The notes were all the same, and were always addressed to Grant, anyway.

Patrols usually didn't bother looking for them.

Alemdra went slowly to Devin's side and knelt. Hunched over the body, she brushed tenderly at Devin's hair, speaking in a soothing tone—the kind one uses with a child, or the very sick. Her shoulders began to rise and fall again with sobs she could no longer hold back.

Tahn stepped forward and put an arm around her, trying this time to be strong.

"It gets inside." Alemdra tapped her chest. "You can't ever really get out of the Scar, can you? Even if you leave." She looked up at Tahn. Her expression said she wanted to be argued with, convinced otherwise.

Tahn could only stare back. He'd gotten out of the Scar—a little bit, anyway—during his time in Aubade Grove. Maybe.

This time, Alemdra *did* look for the note. It wasn't hard to find. But when she unfolded the square of parchment, it *was* different. No words at all. A drawing of a woman, maybe forty or so, beautifully rendered with deep laugh lines around her eyes and mouth, and a biggish nose. Devin had talent that way. Drawing without making everything dreamlike.

The likeness brought fresh sobs from Alemdra. "It's how she imagined her mother."

That tore at Tahn's fragile bravery. He could see in the drawing hints of Devin as an older woman. Simple thing to want to know a parent's face. *Dead gods, Devin, I'm sorry.*

CHAPTER ONE

THE RIGHT DRAW

"Mercy has many faces. One of them looks like cruelty."
—Reconciliationist defense of the gods' placement
of the Quiet inside the Bourne

TAHN JUNELL RACED north across the Soliel plain, and his past raced with him. He ran in the dark and cold of predawn. A canopy of bright stars shone in clear skies above. And underfoot, his boots pounded an urgent rhythm against the shale. In his left hand, he clenched his bow. In his mind, growing dread pushed away the crush of his recently returned memory. Ahead, still out of sight, marching on the city of Naltus Far . . . came the Quiet.

Abandoning gods. The Quiet. Just a few moon cycles ago, these storied races had been to Tahn just that. Stories. Stories he'd believed, but only in that distant way that death concerned the living. *Their* story told of being herded and sealed deep in the far west and north—distant lands known as the Bourne, a place created by the gods before they'd abandoned the world as lost.

One of his Far companions tapped his shoulder and pointed. "Over there." Ahead on the left stood a dolmen risen from great slabs of shale.

Tahn concentrated, taking care where he put his feet, trying to move without drawing any attention. The three Far from the city guard ran close, their flight over the stones quiet as a whisper on the plain. They'd insisted on bearing him company. There'd been no time to argue.

Through light winds that carried the scent of shale and sage, they ran. A hundred strides on, they ducked into a shallow depression beside the dolmen. In the lee side of the tomb, Tahn drew quick breaths, the Far hardly winded.

"I'm Daen," the Far captain said softly. He showed Tahn a wry smile—acquaintances coming here, now—and put out his hand.

"Tahn." He clasped the Far's hand in the grip of friendship.

"I know. This is Jarron and Aelos." Daen gestured toward the two behind him. Each nodded a greeting. "Now, do you want to tell us why we've rushed headlong toward several colloughs of Bar'dyn?" Daen's smile turned inquiring.

Tahn looked in the direction of the advancing army. It was still a long way off. But he pictured it in his head. Just one collough was a thousand strong. So, several of them . . . *deafened gods!* And the Bar'dyn: a Quiet race two heads taller than most men and twice as broad; their hide like elm bark, but tougher, more pliable.

He listened. Only the sound of heavy feet on shale. Distant. The Bar'dyn beat no drum, blew no horn. The absence of sound got inside him like the still of a late-autumn morning before the slaughter of winter stock.

Tahn looked back at Daen. They had a little while to wait, and the Far captain deserved an answer. "Seems reckless, doesn't it." He showed them each a humorless smile. "The truth? I couldn't help myself."

None of the Far replied. It wasn't condescension. More like disarming patience. Which struck Tahn odd, since the Far possessed an almost unnatural speed and grace. A gods-gift. And their lives were spent in rehearsal for war. Endless training and vigilance to protect an old language.

"I wouldn't even be in Naltus if it weren't for the Quiet." Tahn looked down at the bow in his lap, suddenly not sure what he meant to do. His bow—any bow—was a very dear, very old friend. He'd been firing one since he could hold a deep draw. But his bow against an army? *I might finally have waded too far into the cesspit.*

"We guessed that much," said Daen.

Tahn locked eyes with the Far captain, who returned a searching stare. "Two cycles ago, I was living a happy, unremarkable life. Small town called the Hollows. Only interesting thing about me was a nagging lack of memory. Had no recollection of anything before my twelfth year. Then, not long before I turned eighteen . . . a Sheason shows up."

The Far Jarron took a quick breath.

Tahn nodded at the response. "First day I met Vendanj, I realized stories about the Sheason are true. I saw him render the Will. Move things . . . kill. With little more than a thought."

"Vendanj is a friend of the king's," Daen said. "Not everyone distrusts him."

Tahn gave a weak smile to that. "Well, he arrived just before the Quiet got to *my* town, too."

He then looked away to the southwest, at Naltus, a magnificent city risen mostly of the black shale that dominated the long plains. In the predawn light, it was still an imposing thing to look at. It never gleamed. It didn't light up with thousands of lights as Recityv or any other large city. It didn't bustle with industry and trade. It didn't build reputation with art and culture. But the city itself was a striking place, drawn with inflexible lines. It had a permanence and stoicism about it. The kind of place you wanted to be when a storm hit, where you wouldn't fear wind and hard light. And where rain lifted the fresh scent of washed rock. Altogether different than the Hollows, with its hardwood forests and loam.

What Tahn wouldn't have given for some hard apple cider and a round of lies in the form of Hollows gossip. "Vendanj convinced me to follow him to Tillinghast."

This time it was Aelos who made a noise, something in his throat, like a warning. It reminded Tahn that even the Far people, with their gift for battle, and their stewardship over the Language of the Framers . . . even *they* didn't go to Tillinghast.

"Did you make it to the far ledge?" Daen asked.

Tahn turned and looked in the direction of the Saeculorum Mountains, which rose in dark, jagged lines to the east. Impossibly high. Yes, he'd made it there. He and the few friends who'd come with him out of the Hollows. Though, only *he* had stood near that ledge at the far end of everything. A place where the earth renewed itself. Or used to.

He'd faced a Draethmorte there, one of the old servants of the dissenting god. More than that. He'd faced the awful embrace of the strange clouds that hung beyond the edge of Tillinghast. They'd somehow shown him all the choices of his life—those he'd made, and those he'd failed to make. It was a terrible thing to see the missed opportunity to help a friend. Or stranger. Wrapping around him, those clouds had also shown him the *repercussions* of those choices, possible futures. The heavy burden of that knowledge had nearly killed him.

It ached in him still.

But he'd survived the Draethmorte. And the clouds. And he'd done so by learning that he possessed an ability: to draw an empty bow, and fire a part of himself. He couldn't explain it any better than that. It was like shooting a strange mix of thought and emotion. And it left him chilled to the marrow and feeling incomplete. *Diminished.* At least for a while. Maybe something had happened to him in the wilds of Stonemount. Maybe the ghostly barrow robber he'd encountered there had touched him. Touched his mind. Or soul. Maybe both. Whether the barrow robber or not, something had helped him fire *himself* at Tillinghast. Though he damn sure didn't want to do it again, and had no real idea how to control it, anyhow.

"Yes, we made it to the far ledge," he finally said.

He could tell Daen understood plenty about what lay on the other side of the Saeculorum. But the Far captain had the courtesy not to press.

Tahn, though, found relief in sharing some of what had happened. "Near the top, Vendanj restored my memory. He thought it would help me survive up there."

Jarron glanced at the Saeculorum range. "Did it?"

Tahn didn't have an answer to that, and shrugged.

Daen put a hand on Tahn's shoulder. "The Sheason believed if you survived Tillinghast, you could help turn the Quiet back this time. Meet those who've given themselves to the dissenting god . . . in war." He nodded in the direction of the army marching toward them.

Twice before—the wars of the First and Second Promise—the races of the Eastlands had pushed the Quiet back, avoided the dominion they seemed bent toward. Now, they came again.

"Mostly right," said Tahn, "except all I've been fighting since Tillinghast is a head full of bad memories. For two damn days, I've done nothing but sit around in your king's manor, remembering." His grip tightened on his bow, and he spoke through clenched teeth. "Better to be moving. Better to hold someone . . . or something, accountable for that past."

"Idleness makes memory bitter." Daen spoke it like a rote phrase, like something a mother says to scold a laggard child.

Tahn forced a smile, but the feel of it was manic. "Vendanj was the one who took my memory in the first place. Thought it would protect me . . ."

"From the Quiet," Daen finished. "So you're here with a kind of blind vengeance. Angry at the world. Angry at what you believe are the bad choices of people who care for you."

The wind died then, wrapping them in a sullen silence. A silence broken only by the low drone of thousands of heavy feet crossing the shale plain toward them. Into that silence Tahn said simply, "No."

"No?" Daen cocked his head with skepticism.

"I'm not some angry youth." Tahn's smile softened, and he leveled an earnest look on the Far captain. "If I'm reckless, it's because I'm scared. *And* angry. Do I want to drop a few Quiet with this?" He tapped his bow. "Silent hells, yes. But when I saw them from my window in your king's manor this morning . . . I'll be a dead god's privy hole if I'm going to let the Far meet them without me." He pointed to the Quiet army marching in from the northeast. "An army that's probably here *because* of me."

Daen studied Tahn a long moment. "It's reckless . . . but reasonable." He grinned. "Well, listen to me, will you? I sound as contradictory as a Hollows man." His grin faded to a kind of thankful seriousness. "I'm glad you were awake to see them from your window, Tahn. Somehow our scouts failed to get us word."

He'd been up early, as he always was. To greet the dawn. Or rather, imagine it before it came. Those soft moments were more important to him now than ever. Because images plagued him night and day. Images from Tillinghast. Images from a newly remembered past. Sometimes the images gave him the shakes. Sometimes he broke out in a sweat.

Tahn looked again now into the east, anticipating sunrise. The color of the moon caught his eye. Red cast. *Lunar eclipse.* By the look of it, the eclipse had been full a few hours ago. Secula, the first moon, was passing through the sun's penumbra. He'd seen a full eclipse once in . . . *Aubade Grove!* The memories wouldn't stop. He'd spent several years of his young life in the Grove. A place dedicated to the study of the sky. A community of science. This, at least, was a happy memory.

Does the eclipse have anything to do with this Quiet army?

An interesting thought, but there wasn't time to pursue it. The low drone of thousands of Quiet striding the stony plain was growing louder, closer.

"We'll wait until the First Legion joins us on the shale." Daen spoke with the certainty of one used to giving orders. "Anything we observe, we'll report back to our battle strategists."

They didn't understand Tahn's need to run out to meet this army, any more than his friends would have. Sutter and Mira, especially. Sutter because he'd been Tahn's friend since Tahn had arrived in the Hollows. And Mira because—unless he missed his guess—she loved him. So, he'd sent word of the Quiet's approach, and slipped from the king's manor unnoticed.

"I won't do anything foolish," Tahn assured Daen, and began crawling toward the lip of the depression.

The Far captain grabbed Tahn's arm, the smile gone from his face. "What makes you so eager to die?"

Tahn spared a look at the bow in his hand, then stared sharply back at the Far. "I don't want to die. And I don't want *you* to die because of *me*."

The Far captain didn't let go. "I've never understood man's bloodlust, even for the right cause. It makes him foolish."

Tahn sighed, acknowledging the sentiment. "I'm not here for glory." He clenched his teeth again, days of frustration getting the better of him—memories of a forgotten past, images of possible futures. "But I have to do *something*."

The Far continued to hold him, appraising. Finally, he nodded. "Just promise me you won't run in until we see the king emerge from the wall with the First Legion."

Tahn agreed, and the two crawled to the rim of the depression and peeked over the edge onto the rocky plane. What they saw stole Tahn's breath: more Bar'dyn than he could ever have imagined. The line stretched out of sight, and behind it row after row after row . . . "Dear dead gods," Tahn whispered under his breath. Naltus would fall. Even with the great skill of the Far. Even with the help of Vendanj, and his Sheason abilities.

We can't win. Despair filled him in a way he'd felt only once before—at Tillinghast.

And on they came. No battle cries. No horns. Just the steady march over dry, dark stone. A hundred strides away, closing, countless feet pounded the shale like a war machine. Tahn's heart began to hammer in his chest.

Beside him, Daen spoke in a tongue Tahn didn't understand. The sound of it like a prayer . . . and a curse.

Then he saw something that he would see in his dreams for a very long time. The Quiet army stopped thirty strides from him. The front line of Bar'dyn parted, and a slow procession emerged from the horde. First came a tall, withered figure wrapped in gauzy robes the color of dried blood. *Velle! Silent hells.* The Velle were like Sheason, renderers of the Will, except they refused to bear the cost of their rendering. They drew it from other sources.

The Velle's garments rustled as the wind kicked up again, brushing across the shale plain. Tahn's throat tightened. Not because of the Velle, or at least not the Velle alone, but because of what it held in its grasp: a handful of black tethers, and at the end of each . . . a child no more than eight years of age.

"No," Tahn whispered. He lowered his face into the shale, needing to look away, wanting to deny the obvious use the Velle had of them.

When he looked again, two more Velle had come forward. One was female in appearance, and stood in a magisterial dress of midnight blue. The gown had broad cuffs and wide lapels, and polished black buttons in a triple column down the front. The broadly padded shoulders of the garment gave her an imposing, regal look. The third Velle might have been any field hand from any working farm in the Hollows.

He wore a simple coat that looked comfortable, warm, and well used. His trousers and boots were likewise unremarkable. He didn't appear ill fed. Or angry. He simply stood, looking on at the city as any man might after a long walk.

And in the collective hands of these Velle, tethers to six children. The little ones hunched against their bindings. Ragged makeshift smocks hung from their thin shoulders. Each gust of wind pulled at the loose, soiled garments, revealing skin drawn tight over ribs, and knobby legs appearing brittle to the touch.

Worst of all was the look in the children's faces—haunted and scared. And scarred. A look he knew. A look resembling the one worn by many of the children from the Scar. A desolate place he'd only recently remembered. A place where he'd spent a large part of his childhood. Learning to fight. To distrust. Lessons of the abandoned.

Not every memory of the Scar had been bad, though. A name and face flared in his mind: Alemdra. But the bright memory of her quickly changed. Old grief became new at the thought of a ridge where they'd run to watch the sunrise, and seen a friend end her days. *Devin.* Some wounds, he realized, simply couldn't be healed. No atonement was complete enough.

The Velle yanked at the fetters, gathering the small ones close on each side. The children didn't yelp or complain, though grimaces of pain rose in a few faces. Mostly, they fought to keep their balance and avoid falling hard on the shale.

Then the Velle reached down and wrapped their fingers around the wrists of the young ones.

The Far king's legion hadn't emerged from the city wall. The siege on Naltus hadn't yet begun. But Tahn knew the attack these Velle were preparing, fueled by the lives of these six children, would be catastrophic. Naltus might be destroyed before a single sword was raised.

Beside him, the Far captain cursed again and crept down to the dolmen to consult with his fellows. *What do I do?* His grip tightened on his bow. The tales of lone heroes standing against armies were author fancies. Fun to read, but wrong. All wrong. He could get off a few shots at the renderers before any of the Bar'dyn could react. But that wouldn't be enough to stop them, or save the children.

Each Velle raised a hand toward Naltus. Tahn had to do something. Now.

Without thinking further, he climbed onto the shale plain and stood, setting his feet. He pulled his bow up in a smooth, swift motion as he drew an arrow.

Softly he began, "I draw with the strength of my arms, but release as the Will—"

He stopped, not finishing the words he'd spoken all his life when drawing his bow, words taught to him by his father, to seek the rightness of his draw. The rightness of a kill. His father and Vendanj had meant for him to avoid of wrongfully killing anything, or anyone, because they'd thought one day they might need him to go to Tillinghast, where his chances of surviving were better if he went untainted by a wrong or selfish draw.

For as long as he could remember, he'd uttered the phrase and sensed the quiet confirmation that what he aimed at should die. Or not. Usually it was only an elk to stock a meat cellar. But not always. In his mind he saw the Bar'dyn that had stood over his sister Wendra, holding the child she'd just given birth to. He saw himself drawing his bow at it, feeling his words tell him *not* to shoot the creature. He'd followed that impression, and it had cankered his relationship with her ever since.

He was done with the old words. The Velle should die. He wanted to kill them. But he also knew he'd never take them all down. Not even with his ability to shoot a part of himself—something he hadn't learned to control. He'd never be able to stop their rendering of the little ones.

More images. Faces he'd forgotten. Faces of older children— thirteen, fourteen—reposed in stillness. Forever still. Still by their own hands. The despair of the Scar had taken all their hope . . . like Devin, and his failure to save her.

And what of the young ones in these Velle's hands? The ravages of *their* childhood? Long nights spent hoping their parents would come and rescue them. The bone-deep despair reserved for those who learn to stop hoping. He also sensed the ends that awaited each of them. The blinding pain that would tear their spirit from their flesh and remake it into a weapon of destruction. And they wouldn't simply die. Their souls would be spent. If there was a next life, if they had family waiting there, these little ones would never find it. They'd have ceased to be.

Sufferings from his past.

This moment of suffering.

A terrible weight of sorrow and discouragement.

Then a voice in his mind whispered the unthinkable. An awful thing. An irredeemable thing. He fought it. Silently cried out against it. But the dark logic wouldn't relent. And the Velle were nearly ready.

He took a deep breath, adjusted his aim only slightly. And let fly his awful mercy.

The arrow sailed against the shadows of morning and the charcoal hues of this valley of shale. And the first child dropped to the ground.

Through hot, silent tears, Tahn drew fast again, and again. It took the Quiet a few moments to understand what was happening. And when they finally saw Tahn standing beside the dolmen in the grey light of predawn, they appeared momentarily confused. Bar'dyn jumped in front of the Velle like shields. *They still don't understand.*

Like scarecrows—light and yielding—each child fell. Tahn did not miss. Not once.

When it was done, he let out a great, loud cry, the scream ascending the morning air—the only vocal sound on the plain.

Bar'dyn began rushing toward him. Tahn sank to his knees, dropped his bow, and waited for them. He watched the Quiet come as he thought about the wretched thing he'd just done.

It didn't matter that he knew he'd offered the children a greater mercy. Nor that he'd decided this for himself. In those moments, it didn't even matter if what he'd done had saved Naltus.

These small ones, surprise on their faces—*Or was it hope when they saw me? They thought I was going to save them*—before his arrows struck home.

The shale trembled as the Bar'dyn rushed toward him, wearing their calm, reasoning expressions. Already he wondered what he'd do if he had these shots to take again. The bitterness overwhelmed him, and he suddenly yearned for the relief the Bar'dyn would offer him in a swift death. Then strong hands were dragging him backward by the feet, another set of hands retrieving his bow. The Far cast him into the safety of the dolmen. He flipped over and watched Daen Far captain and his squad defend the entrance to the barrow as Bar'dyn rushed in on them.

Jarron fell almost immediately, leaving Daen and Aelos to fight three Quiet.

Tahn couldn't stop trembling. And it had nothing to do with the battle about to darken the Soliel with blood. It was about the way the Quiet would wage their war. About what men would have to do to fight back. Choices like he'd just made.

Abruptly, the Bar'dyn stepped aside. The two Far shared a confused look, their swords still held defensively before them. Then one of the Velle came slowly into view. It stopped and peered past the Far, into the dolmen.

"You're too consumed by your own fear, Quillescent. Rough and untested, despite surviving Tillinghast." Its words floated on the air like a soft, baneful prayer. "Have you learned what you are? What you should do?"

Its mouth pressed into a grim line.

Tahn shook his head in defiance and confusion. Whatever Tillinghast had proven to Vendanj about Tahn being able to stand against the Quiet, the thought of his own future seemed an affliction. He'd rather not know.

"You are a puppet, Quillescent. Or were. But you've cut your strings, haven't you? Killing those children. And for us, you—"

A stream of black bile shot from the creature's mouth, coating its ravaged lips and running down its chin. A blade ripped through its belly. As it fell, it raised a thin hand toward him, and a burst of energy threw Tahn back against one of the tall dolmen stones. Blood burst from his nose and mouth. Shards of pain shot behind his eyes. In his back, the bruising of muscle and bone was deep and immediate.

He dropped to the ground, darkness swimming in his eyes. But he saw Daen and Aelos and the Bar'dyn all look fast to the left, toward the whispering sound of countless feet racing across the shale to meet the Quiet army—the Far legion come to war.

ABOUT THE AUTHOR

PETER ORULLIAN has worked at Xbox for over a decade, which is good, because he's a gamer. He's toured internationally with various bands and been a featured vocalist at major rock and metal festivals, which is good, because he's a musician.

He's also learned when to hold his tongue, which is good, because he's a contrarian.

Peter has published several short stories, which he thinks are good. *The Unremembered* and *Trial of Intentions* are his first novels, which he hopes you will think are good. He lives in Seattle, where it rains all the damn time. He has nothing to say about that. Visit Peter at: www.orullian.com

20174415R00117

Made in the USA
Middletown, DE
18 May 2015